Showtime

A Workplace Novella

Stefanie DiDominzio

Front cover design by Stefanie DiDominzio & Lacey
Burgess.

The Amazon Endure typeface was designed by
2K/DENMARK in 2025.
Template id: ST-414D415A-25-A01

Printed in The United States.
ISBN: 979-8-9916335-1-2

www.stefaniedidominzioauthor.com

DEDICATION

To all the theater kids, drama kids, music kids, and any other creative types that fight through creating art while trying to build lasting relationships.

CONTENTS

ACKNOWLEDGMENTS

This book would not have been possible without the support of my family, especially my fiancé, who endured countless hours of listening to me typing away on my loud keyboard.

This page wouldn't be complete without thanking my friends, my co-workers, and my students. My co-workers are a crazy big family of diverse individuals that laugh together, argue, and cry together, but ultimately make my job worth every minute.

On top of that, the students in my classroom, and those I know just from the hallways, impact me daily. The love and support I get from students is always overwhelming. Some just enjoy my class, some enjoy the ease of passing if they just complete their work, some just need someone to talk to, while others dive into my books and show so much enjoyment in reading.

Special thanks to Y.A. for always volunteering to read my last book to her class during free time. Another special thanks to the students who all purchased and read my last book (Cleanup Crew), many of them while in my classroom. A.J., H.J.G., A.R., and C.W. all loved my book, though we all enjoyed watching A.J. throw the book when she got to a certain part ;) and we all pushed her for days to just keep reading!

I doubt these kids know how much they encourage me to keep teaching and to keep writing! My first year with 8th graders was one to remember.

CHAPTER 1
WELCOME

When the curtain opens, and the show begins, life stops. Actors, singers, dancers, musicians all spend their lives creating, but when they step on the stage to perform, or to become a character, their lives stop.

Welcome to the Show

"We're so happy to have you," the manager announces as she leads me through the theme park. "The 'Iconic Acts' show is in the theater in the middle of the park. It's easy to get to before the park opens, afterwards you'll be fighting the roller coaster crowds."

"And we're expected to arrive before opening?" I ask, trying to remember everything I read from the onboarding paperwork.

"Correct," she answers. "Once you clock in for the day, everyone does morning rehearsal together before showtime."

"And our first show is when?" I ask, glancing at my watch. I'm starting to feel a bit nervous about performing with the group for the first time today after a brief rehearsal.

"Noon, then three, and finally, seven."

"What exactly happened to the last lead singer?" I dare to ask, wondering why she left so suddenly. How else did I get hired from an online video and asked to start work immediately upon my arrival?

The manager stops walking, turning to face me. She looks stern for the first time since I met her a few short minutes ago. "She had her heart broken by the piano player."

"Wait, really?" I ask, wondering why she's so stern about this miniscule fact.

"I'm not allowed to discuss the details, but she was a bit delusional about his possible affection for her. She made a whole stink about him not loving her before she finally blew up on him, while on stage, in the middle of a performance. Her last."

"Well, that's... a lot," I shrug.

"Don't fall for the piano player," she says before turning towards the theater before us. "This is it."

Looking up at the building, I'm not immediately impressed. It looks like an indoor restaurant that no one will enter unless it's raining. And lucky for me, they're calling for storms just before my debut performance today.

"Here we go," the manager cheers with excitement as she opens the door, leading me into the staff entrance of the backstage area. "I hope you're ready to meet everyone! They really are a tight group."

Stepping onto the stage, I am impressed with the size. It's larger than I expected from outside. It has a fantastic lighting system based on numerous rows of rigging. I see several smart lights that I wouldn't expect to see in such a small theater inside of a theme park. "Moving lights? Fancy," I comment while looking around in awe.

"The show really is that good. They have the highest budget in the theme park, other than roller coaster fees and maintenance, for obvious safety reasons," she laughs.

"Wow. No pressure," I feel a nervous laugh escape just as two people step out onto stage. The two males are laughing about something but abruptly stop when they see us.

"Thomas, Johnny, perfect timing," the manager smiles as she walks over to them. "This is Gina, your new lead singer!" her smile lights up the room, but it doesn't help to calm my nerves.

The first male smiles and steps forward, reaching his hand out towards me, "Thomas, your male co-part."

I reach out to shake his hand and feel at ease already in his presence.

The other male steps up, "Johnny, the drummer," he smiles as he extends his own hand.

"Pleasure," I say as I shake Johnny's hand.

"I'll leave you all to meet and greet, rehearse, and get to know one another," the manager says as she begins to back up, heading towards the exit.

"That's it?" I apparently ask out loud.

"Yeah," Johnny sighs. "They really let us do our own thing.

Other than our stage manager yelling for curtain time, we're on our own."

"Good to know," I whisper, suddenly feeling anxious all over again.

"Nervous?" Thomas asks as Johnny steps away towards the drum set at the back edge of the stage.

"Just... a lot," I admit.

Thomas smiles, "Listen. They hired you, so I bet you can sing your ass off."

I smile, trying to contain a laugh.

"The rest is easy. The blocking is super simple. And we're all here for you. If you step in the wrong place, or sing the wrong words, it doesn't matter. We all have your back and will cover for you. The show must go on and all, but we're all here to support one another. This team is amazing, and we're all looking forward to getting to know you."

"Wow," I smile, unsure of what to say next.

"Too much?" Thomas asks, smiling awkwardly. "I'm sorry. Yeah, that was too intense for a hello, nice to meet you type of moment," he drags his hands back aggressively through his hair.

"No," I say, waiting for him to relax before continuing. "That was probably exactly what I needed to hear."

"Really?" he asks.

"Really," I nod. "I'm completely terrified about being here. About showing up and performing, in like two hours. Shit, I haven't even met everyone yet. So, yes, that was what I needed to hear. I'm probably going to mess everything up or, or fall on my face, or forget the words to the songs we've all known since we were children. So, to hear that I'm not going to be alone while I fall on my face, sounds pretty fantastic."

"I think you're going to fit right in here," he smiles. "Let's go meet everyone else." He gestures toward stage right, "After you."

CHAPTER 2
THE CAST

To an audience, the cast members of a show are simply the characters they portray. They are the well thought out characters, reciting the planned lines, while following the directions given by the director. They speak, they sing, and they dance. They are an escape from reality while inside of a theater or on a stage.

What most audience members don't know... the drama that happens backstage, behind the curtain. Drama with drama nerds? No way, right? Wrong. So. Very. Wrong.

Who's Who

"Everyone, gather up," Thomas yells once we're off the stage and in the back hallway. "Meet in the greenroom. Our new leading lady has arrived."

"Must we call me that?" I ask shyly.

Thomas simply shrugs before glancing over his shoulder. "It's what you are my dear. And to be honest, they all knew you were coming today, so it's no big surprise or anything."

"Devon is running late," a male says as he steps into the hallway in front of us.

"Big surprise," Thomas rolls his eyes. "Jimmy, this Is Gina. Gina, this is Jimmy, our guitarist."

"I can pretty much rewrite any of the songs that we perform, so if you get bored, just let me know. We can improve the entire show even."

I reach out to grasp his extended hand, "Good to know."

"That's the musician's room and sound lab." Thomas points out. "Sometimes they record for fun between shows."

Another male steps out as we pass the room. "I'm Robert,

bass," he says with a wave as he heads towards the stage. "I'll get Johnny," he tells Thomas before disappearing towards the stage.

"Robert likes to try to keep everyone in line. We let him manage our time and such because he's just naturally good at it." Thomas continues down to the next hallway, which splits off into two doorways. "This is our hallway. Your room is on the right, mine's on the left."

"We get our own rooms?" I'm surprised by this revelation. Usually, small shows like this get a tiny closet to get ready in.

"Sure do. You can go check it out and put your stuff down if you'd like," Thomas suggests.

"Later," I wave it off. "I'd rather meet everyone and get that over with. Nerves will get the better of me if I start to overthink my life choices."

"Understood," he says knocking on the next door before cracking it open. "Ladies. Meeting. Greenroom. Two minutes." He closes the door gently before glancing at me. "The dancers hang out in there. There's four of them. All sweet girls. They're trying to pad their resumes before they graduate college."

"Smart idea. Do they stick around for long?" I ask.

"Most stay on for at least a year or two. It just depends on their class schedules and other job offers," Thomas explains as he steps into the final room at the end of the hallway. "This, is our green room," he gestures around.

"These digs are pretty on point for an amusement park," I admit as I spin around in the large gathering space. There are tables and chairs for meals or meetings, but also couches, TVs, a huge refrigerator and separate freezer, a few gaming systems, and a row of laptops.

"This show brings in a lot of money somehow. I'd avoid asking, I don't ask questions when they keep giving us money," Thomas shrugs as he sits on one of the nearby couches.

"Other than the dancers, have I met everyone else?" I ask, wondering how large the cast really is.

"Kyle, our stage manager and technical engineer all in one, won't be here until thirty minutes before showtime. He works at a restaurant for breakfast for some extra cash. We run a tight ship, so he's really only needed to push the light cues and keep the mics working."

"Jack of all trades?"

"Pretty much. He's been known to give a few suggestions and hang out with us between shows. Usually, the poor kid is napping. I don't know when he has time for class and homework."

"Anyone else I need to know about?"

"The girls should be here soon. The only other person is Devon."

"The one who's late?" I ask, remembering someone mention that name.

"The one and only."

"And he's the...."

"Pianist," Thomas answers. "And the player of the cast."

"He plays, what? Something besides the piano?" I'm lost at his statement.

Thomas leans forward and whispers, "He's what the ladies call a player."

"Oh, you mean he's... Got you. He's *that* guy."

Thomas leans back before whispering, "Just don't mention it in front of the dancers."

As if on cue, the four dancers walk in. The first is a beautiful black female with gorgeous long hair. "Hey. I'm Taylor!" she says with an energetic voice. She opens the fridge to retrieve a drink before making her way to a chair at one of the tables.

"Amanda," the next dancer says as she nods before taking a seat away from everyone. She's a brunette supporting a moody temper, but I'll hold off judgements until I really get to know everyone.

"She's not really a morning person," the blonde female whispers as she walks by. She then turns and walks backwards as she waves to me, "I'm Alice, by the way."

The last female, another brunette sits by the door and doesn't pass by me. "Hey girl. I'm Meredith," she says before looking back down at her cellphone and typing away.

"Meredith strives to be a social media marketer, so she's always on her phone," Alice commentates.

Thomas stands, "Ladies, this is Gina." The musicians I've already met walk in from the other end of the room where a door leads directly toward the attached restaurant. "Does anyone have any comments, complaints, or suggestions before we prepare for rehearsal?"

"Um, yeah," Alice raises her hand. "Where's Devon?"

"Running late," Robert replies with an annoyed eye roll.

"Must have over*slept* again," Amanda adds. Clearly there is a lot left unsaid in this moment.

"Gina, Meredith is the official understudy for your part, so she'll run you through the blocking real quick before we start rehearsal. We'll run the entire show and see how it goes. Then we can make adjustments as necessary before our first show at noon," Thomas adds before heading towards the hallway.

"I'm totally on it," Meredith says as she springs up from her seat. "You ready?"

"As ready as I'll ever be," I shrug with a forced smile.

∞

Meredith walks me through some very simple blocking for each song. She says to just watch out for everyone else but do whatever I need to, to get through the day. There isn't much required of anyone other than where to stand for the beginning of a song. The dancers, of course, have some complicated choreography, but that won't interfere with my blocking as long as I don't try to walk through them.

Once she's done, we run the show as a full cast. Well, mainly. Shortly after we run the show, the mysterious piano player finally shows up.

"Did we have a planned run through?" he asks, as soon as he walks in just as we finish the finale.

"Obviously," Amanda says in a sassy tone before storming off.

"Remember that our new female lead singer starts today," Thomas adds in, gesturing towards where I stand next to him.

"Oh, shit. I totally forgot," he sounds genuine, but I'm not so sure I trust anything he says or does based on the small amount I know.

"Thankfully, you're not entirely necessary," Meredith smirks as Devon runs up the steps and past her onto the stage.

Devon approaches me with his hand stretched out, "I'm Devon. Sorry I wasn't here."

I reluctantly shake his hand. "Gina."

"Like Meredith said, thankfully you're not entirely necessary," Robert adds.

"Is that a threat?" Devon perks up.

"Ladies, ladies," Johnny walks between them. "Stop it. You're both pretty. And... let's not scare off the new girl on day one, okay?"

"I'm just trying to have some fun," Johnny bops his shoulders as he walks backwards toward his drum set. "Not my fault Devon woke up on the wrong side of the bed this morning," he shrugs.

"Sorry Gina. I promise, we're actually all really good friends," Devon apologies.

"Really, really, good friends," Amanda says in a sarcastic tone before walking off stage.

"Amanda," Alice runs after her, sounding concerned.

"Well, that's the show folks," Thomas tries to break the awkward tension. "How do you feel Gina?"

"As good as I can considering I have to do it for an audience in just less than an hour," I shrug.

"You'll do just fine," Devon says, patting me on the shoulder before sticking his headphones back over his ears and walking away towards the back hallway.

"You're gonna to do amazing," Thomas smiles, trying to help boost my confidence after that odd banter between everyone.

∞

An hour later, the lights come up, the band starts playing, and the show goes off without a hitch. I remember most of the blocking and just stay out of the way the rest of the time. The show is even better with the costumes and an energetic audience. The storms outside began just before showtime, driving in a full house of people. It was a bit overwhelming at first, but as the show went on, I slowly felt more and more relaxed.

∞

One on One

After the crowd leaves, I find myself looking out at the empty tables. Thomas walks over and sits down on the edge of the stage next to me and sighs, "See. That wasn't so bad, was it."

"I didn't fall on my face as anticipated, so, not too bad," I smile.

"Any questions?" he asks.

"Yeah, but not exactly about the show," I admit.

"Gossip time?" he asks with a smirk.

"Give me the low down. Who's sleeping with who? Who secretly hates someone? Who isn't really my friend? Everything. I want it all."

"Getting straight to it?" he shakes his head.

"We can skip ahead to what really happened with the girl I'm replacing," I shrug, biting my lower lip in anticipation of his reaction.

His lip smack, "That's complicated."

"Give me the highlights," I nudge him with my elbow to show him this doesn't need to be a serious moment.

He sighs, looking around to be sure we're alone before he explains. "Short version?"

I nod, leaning in to hear.

"As I said, Devon can be a bit of a... player," he shrugs. "That being said, our former leading lady may have created a narrative for them in her mind that led to her breaking her own heart."

"So, Devon didn't sleep with her?" I ask.

"According to Devon, she was really pushy about them being a forever couple. He told her that wasn't in the cards for them. From then on, he claims to have kept his distance. The problem was, she never stopped talking about him."

"She drove herself crazy?" I theorize.

"Either she truly believed the stories she was telling, or she wanted it to be true so badly that she went too far with it. Either way, she got really clingy at the end. She kept running up to him after shows and hugging him. She told everyone they were getting married even."

"What did Devon have to say to that?"

Thomas laughs as he glances around again. "Devon responded by blasting her on social media. He was able to record her telling the dancers about their nuptials. He then posted it on all of his socials saying that she was insane and needed mental help."

"He didn't exactly fix the issue," I say as I stand, stretching my back.

"You're right in that assessment," Thomas sighs before standing and staring at me as if he has more to say.

"What? Out with it," I encourage.

"I may not agree with the way he did it, but it had to be done."

"Would you have handled it differently, if it had been you in his shoes?" I ask, curious about his character.

He runs his fingers back through his hair before beginning to walk away. After a few steps, he stops to turn towards me. "I'd like to think that I could have stopped the behavior before it got too far. The problem was, none of us knew she'd take it to the extent that she did. She broke apart a family. We all tried to help her, but she wasn't going to allow anyone to change her mind. So, no. I don't think I could have done anything differently. I hope that I never have to try."

"Is it good that she's gone?"

"She was a good singer. She was a decent fit here, until she went off the deep end. In reality, she was never meant to be here. She only got the part because their first choice got an internship at Universa-world instead."

"So, the part of your leading lady has yet to truly be filled?" I dare to ask, hoping my question doesn't cross some line.

He smiles before looking down at the ground, shaking his head. "I haven't allowed myself to have a relationship in a very long time."

"You don't show it on stage," I smile at my attempt at a complaint.

He glances up and returns my smile. "The motivation for my character is to get the girl in the end."

"And maybe you shall," I smile as I walk down the stairs that lead down to the audience tables and the coffee shop across the building.

CHAPTER 3
MOTIVATION

Real actors, they need a reason to be. They need to understand what motivates their characters. Why do they think the way they do. Why do they act the way they do. Why do they say the things that they say. Without motivation, they are doing something very, very wrong.

Human beings, real people, are also driven by their own personal motivations. Even without knowing it, human beings follow their personal motives to compete in the journey of life. Some people are super competitive and are motivated to win. Some people just want to prove themselves. Others are just trying to survive. So, what is your motivation?

Devon

Ten minutes before the doors open for the audience, I walk out onto stage to pace. One of my pre-show traditions is to pace around the space to prepare myself and get into the right headspace. I never expected to find Devon lightly keying the piano. He doesn't notice me at first. I watch as he lightly strokes each key as he plays a soft melody that I'm unfamiliar with. His eyes are closed as he leans into each movement, feeling the music as if it's a part of him. He must sense my presence since he suddenly stops playing and opens one eye to peer at me.

He sits up straighter and pulls his headphones off his head, sliding them around his neck as he smiles, "Didn't see you there."

"I'm sorry," I gesture around. "I didn't mean for you to stop."

He shakes his head. "No worries. The house is about to open anyways," he gestures toward the audience as he stands.

"Five minutes," Kyle yells from the booth upstairs.

"Thanks Kyle," Devon yells up before stepping away from the piano bench and meeting me center stage.

"You have a gift," I whisper.

"What's that?" he asks as he scrunches his eyebrows together.

"Piano. You have a natural talent."

"And you know this from one set?" he shakes his head in confusion.

"I know this from watching you a minute ago. It's in your bones. People would kill for that natural talent."

"Uh-huh," he grunts before shaking his head and beginning to walk away.

"Devon?" I stop him before he can get backstage.

"Yeah?" he looks over his shoulder at me.

"What's your deal?"

He smiles before turning to walk back towards center stage. "How do you mean?"

"Why are you here? What do you want out of life? I don't know," I shrug. "Anything."

"I'm here to pay the bills. I'm here to play music. I want to *make* music. My *own* music. But that's more difficult than I anticipated. So, I'm here, having a good time, entertaining, and just playing."

"Double meaning there?" I ask, wondering if I've gone too far.

He laughs before biting his lower lip and watching me for several moments before glancing toward the ground, avoiding eye contact. "Not everything you hear is true, you know?"

"Enlighten me. Pretend I know zero."

"I didn't have a relationship with our former leading lady. I never touched her. I never dated her. Nothing," he sounds defensive, but not aggressive as he explains.

"But, with others?"

He steps closer to be sure I can hear his hushed words as he whispers, "What's it to you?"

"Curiosity killed the cat. I don't want to be the cat. I want to be the wolf, seeing all and ruling my part of the woods."

"Interesting metaphor."

"Changing the subject?"

"I don't do anything on a whim. Everything I do has a plan and a preferred outcome. Sometimes, those outcomes don't take form. Sometimes I have to give up and move on."

"So, what you're saying is, you've played the field?"

"Ain't no business, like show business," he whispers as he turns and jogs off, ducking backstage just before Kyle walks up the steps from the audience.

"House is about to open Gina," Kyle warns before climbing back down the steps.

"Thanks Kyle."

Kyle waves as he walks away, disappearing up the aisle as he heads to open the doors to the theater.

∞

Meredith

"Ready to do it all over again?" Meredith asks as she leans around the door frame of my room.

I smile as she pulls me out of my deep thoughts, "The show must go on."

"Ut-oh," she frowns as she swings her body into my room, leaning back against the door frame while crossing her arms in front of her. "Do we need to talk?"

I shake my head and swat at the air. "Oh, no. Nothing like that. I was just zoning out."

"Are you sure?" she raises her eyebrows as if she doesn't believe me.

"I am perfectly happy to be here. I am ready to do the show again."

"Okay," she uncrosses her arms and spins a chair around to sit on it backwards facing me. "Who did you talk to that soured your positive attitude?"

I roll my eyes, turning to face her. "Devon."

"Oh, shit."

"No, no. It wasn't anything like that."

"Like what?" she raises her brows in curiosity.

"I know exactly what he is, or what everyone claims him to be."

"Oh, he is the biggest player there is around here," her tone is final, as if she knows the whole truth.

"That sounds personal."

"Oh, it is," she nods.

"I'm not mad about him or his exploits."

"What did he say?"

"He tried to avoid the subject. I asked him why he was here. Somehow, we got on the topic of his history with women. He said

13

that everything he does has been planned and executed. He says that's just part of show business and then walked off like it was no big deal," I shrug and shake my head, not sure how to react to his words.

"Wow. Yeah, that sounds like Devon."

"I'm guessing you two didn't work out?"

She smiles, "Devon and I flirted for a long time. I really wanted there to be more. We used to spend lunch together after the first show. Then we'd work together in the musician studio after the second show."

"You're into music too?"

She nods with a shy smile. "We were writing a song. It started out as just a casual working relationship until the song turned into something more. It became deeply emotional. We both grew feelings that we weren't ready for; that we didn't understand. Neither of us had those feelings for one another. It just sort of blossomed out of the experience, writing the song."

"Did you guys ever talk about it?"

"No," she looks down at the floor. "We kept working on the song. We recorded it. We… well we had another experience together."

"What happened with the song?"

"We decided to set it aside."

"For now? Or for good?" I ask.

She finally looks up and forces a partial smile. "We didn't really discuss a possible timeline."

"Did you… did you sleep with him?"

She rolls her lips together, glances away and nods.

"Oh, Meredith. I'm sorry. Is that what ruined the song?"

She shakes her head. After a moment, she takes a deep breath and looks up at the ceiling. "Alice ruined it."

"Alice? The other dancer?"

She nods.

"She came in a few days later bragging about finally getting Devon to go home with her."

"Oh, shit. I'm sorry."

She shakes her head, wiping away a few tears that sneak out of her lashes. "I should have known better."

"You can't deny feelings when they develop, especially in the way they did while writing a song."

"Doesn't mean I shouldn't have given in to my desires," she wipes more tears before standing up and stretching.

"Sometimes things like that just happen. It's show business. We're an emotional crowd. We have our own feelings and emotions, along with the characters we pretend to be."

"Does that make it right?" she asks.

"It makes it normal."

"I guess it could be worse," she giggles at a joke I'm not privy to.

I raise my brows and stare at her until she realizes I'm missing something.

"It could be worse. I could have made it all up like the idiot you replaced," she breaks out into laughter before she can even finish her sentence.

"Wow."

"Too soon?" she asks through uncontrollable laughter.

"Fifteen minutes," Thomas pops in to announce. He notices Meredith's behavior and appears concerned when he looks at me and asks, "Is she crying?"

I shrug, "I'm honestly not sure."

"Oh, you two!" she continues laughing and crying all at once. "You're hilarious."

Thomas and I exchange a confused stare as Meredith hugs me through her tears.

"I'm going to change for the show," she says as she walks past Thomas to exit the room.

"What was that about?" Thomas asks.

"I don't think I even know, honestly."

"Ready for another show?" he asks, getting back to the topic at hand.

"As ready as I'll ever be."

∞

Johnny

With five minutes left, I walk into the back hallway and pace back and forth. It's not the same as my preshow stage pace, but sometimes routines need to adjust to new settings. After a few paces, I notice Johnny is air drumming a song with his drum sticks in the doorway to the stage.

He notices me pacing and stops, "Hey Gina."

"Johnny," I reply, coming to a stop near the doorway.

He steps out and leans against the wall on the opposite side of the doorway. "Still okay with being here?"

I laugh, "It's only been one show."

"Yeah, but you've met everyone, and there's a lot of personality going around in here," he gestures to our surroundings.

"Touche."

"Everyone being welcoming?" he asks after a beat of silence.

"Mainly."

"Someone isn't?"

I roll my eyes, but don't say anything.

Moments later Devon flings open a door across the hall and bops his way down the hall dramatically to whatever music is playing in those headphones. "Johnny," he yells with a nod as he passed between us onto the stage.

"Ah, Devon," is all Johnny has to say.

"How do you do it?"

"Do what exactly?" he asks, turning back to me as he leans his left arm against the door frame.

"Be so relaxed and chill while still playing a show like this after all these years?"

"Are you calling me old?" he raises his brows.

"Oh, no. I didn't mean... Shit," I begin to panic.

"Relax, I'm kidding," Johnny smiles.

"That's not funny," I pout.

He shrugs. "For me, this show brings home money for doing a job I actually love. I remember the days fighting for better paying gigs and touring the country, shit, the world. But then I met Airabeth. She wanted something more stable once we decided that we both wanted kids. So, we dug deep into our finances and decided that it would be tough for a few years, but that her career would provide the best money and the insurance so that I could keep playing and doing what I love, without the big checks and constant tour schedule changes."

"Wow. Johnny, that's beautiful."

He smiles. "I'd have given it up. I'd get a boring desk job or factory work to make it work with Airabeth. But I was lucky. I found a partner that cared that we were both happy."

"That is a beautiful and rare thing."

"So, to answer your question... I get to do what I love every day without any stress. Then, I get to go home to my beautiful wife and my children every single night."

"Sounds like a dream come true," I smile.

"It's my dream come true," Johnny smiles.

"Showtime!" Kyle says as he walks into the hallway. He proceeds to walk down the hall, yelling "Showtime," into every door as he goes.

"Guess that's our cue," Johnny smiles and nods before disappearing backstage.

Thomas walks out of our hallway and smiles when he notices I'm already at the stage door. "Ready?" he asks.

"Ready to rock their socks off," I say in a sassy voice.

"Alright! Let's do this," he says as his hand grazes my lower back to lead me through the stage door.

CHAPTER 4
THE AFTER SHOW

College kids, party hard. Frat kids, party hard. Theater kids, they party harder. Dancers dance harder. Singers, they karaoke longer. And drinking, well they're all going to throw down harder than any other college party.

School is over and they're part of the real world? Some things never change. Perform all day. Party all night.

Friday Night

"Gina! You made it!" Meredith yells and runs my way, beer sloshing over the edge of her disposable cup.

"I talked her into it," Thomas smiles from over my shoulder.

"Oh, look at you!" Meredith yells.

"How much have you had to drink?" I ask.

"Guuuurl. I'm in college. You think I keep count?" Meredith giggles before scampering off.

"Well, that was unexpected," I turn to Thomas to gauge his reaction.

"Guess I should have warned you that the dancers party hard before anyone else even arrives," Thomas shrugs.

"College kids?"

"College kids," he nods.

"Johnny? Robert?" I ask.

Thomas laughs. "You won't catch them dead at these things. Even for the new girl."

"Wow," I say, covering my heart with my hand. "I'm hurt."

"Dramatic, I like it," Thomas smiles at me. "Drink?"

"Please!" I answer, knowing this night won't be like I expected.

"Gina! Over here!" Alice yells from the next room.

I smile and follow her voice. "Hey."

Taylor runs over and wraps her arm around my neck. "Gina," she whispers. "I'll warn you now. Meredith and Alice are lushes. Whatever you do, do *not* try to keep up. You'll fail! Then you'll have to drop out."

"You know that I'm already years past graduation, right?" I ask.

Taylor begins to laugh, "Right! I forgot!" She lets go of me and stumbles back towards the couch, flopping down onto it without any grace.

"College kids," Thomas reminds me as he hands me a drink over my shoulder.

∞

Saturday Night

"Do you know what tomorrow is?" Devon asks as we walk up to his front door.

"Sunday?"

"Exactly. No shows on Sundays," Devon reminds me as he unlocks the door.

"And that's relevant because?"

"Everyone parties harder on Saturday nights," he smiles as he shoves his door open. "Here, let me get those," he says as he takes the box of liquor from my arms.

"Thanks," I reply as I step past the threshold of his front door.

"Can you hit the lights," he gestures to the wall next to the door.

I reach over and flip all three switches and am overwhelmed by the size of his apartment. "Wow."

"Yeah," he sounds embarrassed as he places the box on a kitchen counter in the next room. "When you have family money and very few expenses, it's easier to get a nice pad to throw sweet parties at."

"Subtle," I whisper as I follow him into the kitchen.

"No. I wasn't trying to... Listen, my parents died in a car crash when I was a young teenager. They had money. They left it all to me. They never liked my passion for music, so it pushed me towards it. So far, I haven't had much luck producing my own work. Playing at the theme park keeps my talent fresh until I find the right path."

Wow. That was more truth than I expected out of Devon.

He smiles. "Don't tell anyone else that I bore my soul to you. Most of them have no idea."

"Then why tell me?"

He opens a bottle of wine from the fridge and pours us each a glass. He hands one to me and holds his up. "I just feel like I can trust you with my secrets. I know you'll never go after my heart."

"Since you trust me... Can I ask you an honest question? No judgement?"

He downs his wine and places his glass down, contemplating his answer. He leans both elbows onto the counter before deciding. "Shoot."

"What about the song you wrote with Meredith?"

Devon holds his breath for several long moments before blowing it out slowly and roughly running his hand back through his hair. "She told you about that," it's a statement, clearly rhetorical.

"Listen, I didn't mean to pry. I was just curious about it," I try to brush off the topic, but we're stuck.

"No. It's okay that you asked. I just... I can't go back and erase what I did," he confesses.

"What do you mean?"

He sighs deeply before sitting on a bar stool nearby. "Writing that song, it brought out a whole new side of me, of my music. We felt it in our bones. It was... beautiful."

"The music or the connection?" I ask.

He glances over at me before looking back down at his hands. "Both," he admits.

"What really happened?"

"What did she tell you?" he asks.

I laugh as I sit down across from him.

"What's funny?"

"Yesterday you were blowing me off between shows. Everyone said to just keep my distance. Now we're having a heart to heart about you and Meredith."

He nods and smiles, "Yeah, you're right. I'm pretty ridiculous."

"Tell me all about it," I gently push, hoping for the truth.

"Meredith and I were great friends. I even told her when I couldn't make up my mind about Alice and Amanda."

"Alice *and* Amanda?"

"Different story. Different day."

"Right. Go on," I nod in encouragement.

"Meredith would always spend the afternoons in the studio with me. I'd mess around with melodies and sometimes if we liked it, we'd mess around pretending to write lyrics. It surprised both of us when a song came out of it one day."

"Did you record it together?"

He nods. "Yeah. It was the most amazing thing I ever did. Not just the song and the excitement of creating something real... It was her."

"Then what happened?"

He shakes his head. "Alice and Amanda happened," he avoids eye contact.

"Did you run?"

He nods. "I sabotaged myself like I always do."

"Why not fight to get her back?" I ask.

"She said she'd never forgive me. And I can't blame her for that."

"You can build back your friendship. If you can learn to trust one another, you can decide what direction is best for your *friendship*."

"I wish it was that easy."

"Maybe it can be," I encourage.

"Devon?" we hear Thomas yelling from the front door.

"We're in the kitchen," Devon yells back.

"Keep this between us?" Devon asks at a whisper.

"Of course," I smile, placing my hand briefly on his in promise.

"Where is everyone?" Thomas asks, eyeing our hands before either of us can pull away.

"Late," Devon answers before getting up to get Thomas his own wine glass. He then fills all three glasses. "Cheers."

"Cheers," Thomas and I say in sync.

"Party's here!" I hear Taylor yelling as the front door opens and closes.

"No music?" Alice asks as she runs around the corner.

"We were waiting for you," Devon smiles and stares at Alice, following her everyone movement as she enters the living room and begins to mess with his sound system.

"Come on," I gesture for Devon to leave the confines of his kitchen. "Time to get drunk!"

"Oh really?" Thomas asks as he loops his arm through mine,

leading me towards the living room.

"Apparently we have two days off and can all crash here if the night ends badly?"

"Always!" Devon yells as he raises a glass.

"Then time for some cast bonding!" I yell as I raise my glass.

"Cast bonding!" everyone yells, raising their glasses and drinking.

The music gets loud. The drinking games begin. And before we know it, we're all passing out drunk all over the living room.

CHAPTER 5
WEEKEND

Being hung over sucks on workdays, but it sucks even more on the weekends. It sucks even more when you just moved and have to unpack an entire apartment worth of belongings.

Cast bonding brings people together. You can form lasting friendships with the people you work around. These can be your best friends, your work enemies, or even your one show stands. Okay, that doesn't really make sense, right? Or does it? During the run of a show, you get close to the people around you. You form friendships. You grow specific relationships. Sometimes you find a new bestie. But... how many of those friendships last after you move on to the next show? One show stand friendships are a real thing. When you move on to a new town and a new show, friendships often start all over. It's a way to start fresh, but it's also a way to leave friendships behind, even when we promise not to.

Wake Up

"Okay sleepy heads," a male voice yells from the area of the front door as I roll over and groan. "Time for a wakeup call!"

"We brought breakfast," another male voice says.

"And coffee," the first continues. "*Lots* of coffee."

"Why so loud?" Jimmy groans from the corner of the room.

"I think I'm gonna..." Taylor begins before jumping up and sprinting toward the bathroom.

"Someone can't hold their liquor still," one of the males who came in whispers from the kitchen.

I roll over to look, squinting through my lashes as my eyes adjust to the bright sunlight shining through the window.

"Robert?"

"Morning Gina," Robert smiles.

"Why is Robert here?" I roll back over and ask the person sleeping next to me in the middle of the living room floor.

"Robert and Johnny try to make sure we're all still alive after we party too hard on the weekends," Thomas replies.

"Oh shit," I whisper.

"What?" Thomas sits up suddenly, fearing something's wrong.

"Oh, nothing," I shake my head. I can't tell him that I'm just surprised to wake up next to him. "When did we all decide to fall asleep on the floor?" I ask as I try to sit up and stretch my aching back.

"Too late," Thomas says as he rolls over, facing away from the sunlight shining into the kitchen.

"Why do you two always insist on opening my blinds as soon as you get here," Devon groans as he slams down a few of the blinds that were open.

"Because you need some Vitamin D," Robert rolls his eyes as he reopens the blinds, pushing a cup of coffee into Devon's hand.

"Thanks Dad," Devon grumbles as he plops down onto a chair at the kitchen table.

"Is this normal?" I ask, trying to stand without stepping on the other bodies littering the floor.

"Unfortunately," Devon admits between sips of coffee.

"Here," Johnny says as he hands me my own coffee cup.

"Thanks," I smile, wiping the sleep from my puffy eyes.

"Bagels, pastries, and such are in the box," Robert points. "I'm about to whip up some steak and eggs."

"Steak and eggs?" I ask, wondering if I heard him wrong.

"Robert's making his steak and eggs?" Amanda asks as she stumbles out of Devon's room.

I raise my brows at him as he catches my eye, quickly shaking his head at me before looking away.

"Medium?" Robert asks Amanda as I hear the steaks sizzle as they hit the grease in the pan.

"Don't you know it," Amanda answers with a smile, and a peppy tone. That tone doesn't fit the grumpy chic I've come to know this week.

I turn toward Devon again, raising my brows as I stare his way, sipping my coffee until he glances my way. I gesture towards

Amanda with my eyes, hoping he'll give away his feelings on the subject.

Devon sighs heavily before running his fingers angrily back through his hair. He downs the rest of his coffee, slams his cup down, and storms off into his room; slamming the door behind him.

"He okay?" Johnny asks.

"Regret is a dangerous emotion," I whisper.

Amanda spins to Devon's door before turning to glare at me. "You don't know anything. You just got here," she bites off at me.

I shrug, sipping my coffee. "Just an observation."

"Rain check on the steak Robert," Amanda says before grabbing her coat and purse and storming off toward the front door.

"Medium? Gina?" Robert asks as he flips the steak as if nothing dramatic just went down behind him.

"Medium is perfect," I smile.

"We knew you'd fit right in here," Johnny laughs into his own coffee.

"Right? We needed another grown up around here," Robert adds as he puts his back to the cooktop.

"Speaking of..." Johnny starts, glancing into the living room. "Thomas isn't usually one to drink enough to crash and spend the night."

"Really?" I ask, glancing over at his sleeping form on the living room floor.

"Really," Jimmy admits as he stumbles into the kitchen. "I'm usually the only one other than Devon and the girls."

"Partly because he can't hold his liquor," Johnny teases.

"But mainly because we beg him not to leave the girls alone with Devon," Robert adds before flipping a steak onto a plate next to some eggs. "He takes one for the team," he adds as he places the plate in front of me.

Jimmy grunts as he stuffs a danish into his mouth. "I drank more than usual," he adds.

"Please don't talk with your mouth full," Johnny begs. "You remind me of my five-year-old when you do that."

"Sorry," he says after swallowing down his food. "Thomas and Gina were clearly staying, so I let lose a bit," he shrugs before stuffing another large piece of danish into his mouth.

"Wow," I nod, cutting into my steak.

"It's not easy being the one in charge every weekend," Jimmy adds.

"What exactly are you in charge of?" Thomas asks as he stretches his way into the kitchen.

"How's your back?" I ask.

"Sore isn't a strong enough word," he smiles as he makes his way to the chair next to me.

"We were just telling Gina about my weekly chaperon services," Jimmy whispers before finishing off the danish he's been stuffing down.

"Yeah," Thomas acknowledges. "We do tend to leave him out here alone to keep an eye on the girls."

"After the display we saw this morning, I'm glad you do," I add, glancing at Devon's door.

"Did I already miss the drama this morning?" Thomas asks.

From the cooktop, Robert flips a steak before answering. "Devon was his normal grumpy self until Gina got involved."

"What did you do?" Thomas asks, crossing his arms and giving me a deeply accusatory look.

"Devon was clearly upset about his choices last night," I shrug, avoiding eye contact with everyone. I cut another chunk out of my steak as I go on. "I may have mumbled something about regret while Amanda was within earshot." I quickly stuff the steak into my mouth to prevent me from saying anything more.

"Wow! Vicious," Thomas smiles. "I like it."

"Don't encourage her," Robert hands Thomas a plate of steak and eggs as he stares at him intently. It's like there is something secret passing between them at this moment. I try to decipher it, but before I can Johnny clears his throat, breaking up the moment.

"So, what are you up to today, Gina?" Jimmy breaks the awkward tension.

I groan loudly, causing everyone's head to turn. "I have to unpack. My moving box is being delivered this afternoon."

"Moving Box?" Devon asks as he walks back into the kitchen, fully showered and dressed for the day.

"You know, moving box," I answer. "The freight line moving rentals. It's like a mini freight cart that they drop off for you to pack, then they move it, and drop it at your new location?"

"I thought those had a different name?" Jimmy wonders aloud

as he reaches for another pastry.

"How long do you have to unpack it?" Robert asks.

"I have twenty-four hours until they pick it up. If it's not ready, I get charged an extra day."

"And... you have help?" Jimmy asks.

I shake my head.

"How big is this moving box?" Devon asks.

I scroll through my phone until I find the photo I took when I finished packing it just last week.

"And you think you can unpack that alone in twenty-four hours?" Jimmy asks wide eyed.

I bite my bottom lip, knowing it was a terrible plan from the beginning, but knowing I don't have the money to pay for another day. I shrug, "Cost effective motivation?"

"That's it," Thomas says after dropping his fork once he's finished his last bite of steak.

"What's it?" I ask, looking around to see if anyone else is as confused as me. Everyone else looks as determined as Thomas. "What am I missing here?"

"What time is it coming?" Robert asks.

"Delivery is set for two," I admit reluctantly.

"Add her to the group chat," Johnny directs Thomas.

"On it," Thomas replies, pulling out his phone and quickly doing something.

"Send us the address in the group," Johnny directs me next as he pulls out his phone, dials a number, and holds it up to his ear as it rings. "Hey babe," he says once someone answers, walking away for privacy.

"What's going on right now?" I ask, looking at everyone like they're clearly forgetting to tell me something.

My phone chirps with a new text. "That's the group chat. Welcome," Thomas nods to my phone. "Put the address in there for everyone."

"But why?" I ask, still feeling like I'm missing out on something obvious.

"This is their way of over stepping," Devon whispers.

"I don't get it," I shake my head, looking to him for help.

"Your box will be unpacked within two hours," Devon adds, downing another cup of coffee.

"I doubt my ability to unpack it in twenty-four, let alone two," I shake my head at him in disbelief.

"Gina," Devon says, waiting for me to look up. "We're all going to be there unpacking. That's what's going on here," he gestures around to everyone milling about in his kitchen. "Like I said, they're over stepping. That's what they do. Welcome to the group chat. You're stuck with us now," he nods before placing the coffee mug in the sink and disappearing into another room.

CHAPTER 6
UNBOXING PARTY

Moving sucks. It really doesn't matter if you're a teenager or an adult. Moving just plain sucks. It is so much work. There is so much work to stuff belonging into tiny boxes. There is so much work unpacking and making a new space livable and comfortable to be in. Moving is stressful. Moving is a break in routine and order.

Moving alone is even worse. Packing up everything you own is not much if you're young or do not own much. Once you are an adult and begin to acquire things and necessities, moving gets even more complicated. Picture for example that you like to read. You have a beautiful bookshelf full of your favorites. What do you have on there, one hundred? Two hundred books? Try to pack those. Now, instead of one or two bookshelves, you have twenty-six boxes of books, or more.

That example was only one item, books. Now imagine your bathroom, and those three different types of shampoo that you bought while they were on sale, before you decided to move. What about the kitchen? How many toasters do you need? Actually, how did you end up with three toasters to begin with? Whatever. The point is, packing sucks; unpacking sucks; and moving sucks.

What makes it better? Being rich and paying someone to do it for you. True, but this is reality. And thespians do not make enough money to pay someone to move them. That's just a fact.

The Moving Box

Thankfully the box was delivered an hour early. It gave me the opportunity to figure out what I wanted in each room so that I could easily explain where I wanted the cast, my new best friends, to put everything.

"Coming!" I yell as the front doorbell begins to ring repeatedly.

"Gina!" Thomas smiles as I prop open the front door, gesturing for them to come on in.

"Housewarming gift," Devon hands me two bottles of wine.

"Two?" I'm curious.

Devon shrugs, "I didn't know if you were a red or a white wine kinda gal."

"Depends on the day," I smile back.

"Perfect, now you are prepared for both," he gestures to the bottles before circling around the foyer. "This is a nice place."

"Not as nice as yours," I mention, watching how he really takes in all the details.

"He's got a thing for architecture," Johnny says as he steps into the door.

"I can see that," I whisper. "Why doesn't he just become an architect?"

"Too much math," Johnny laughs. "He prefers to appreciate it, not create it."

"My art is through music, not two by fours," Devon yells from across the kitchen.

"He also has impeccable hearing," Jimmy adds, stepping in next.

"Heard that," Devon yells as he disappears down the hallway.

"For me?" I ask as Jimmy hands me a small square box.

Jimmy smiles, "It's a box of assorted pastries from Johnny's wife. She's planning on opening her own bakery soon, and she loves a chance to recruit future customers."

"Be careful," Johnny says from the hallway. "Her baked goods are like a drug."

"Then how are you not overweight?" Amanda asks while running up to the front door.

"My gym membership," Johnny shrugs before disappearing.

"Thanks for coming," I awkwardly smile at Amanda.

"Yeah," she whispers, looking around to be sure no one is in earshot. She looks down at the ground before continuing. "I agree with what you said."

"Sorry?" I ask, wondering what she's referring to. It can't be about what I said this morning about regret, right?

"I know that Devon regrets last night. I knew he would before we even closed his bedroom door," she continues at a whisper.

"Then…. why?" I ask, unsure of how to word it without being direct.

She looks up into my eyes and forces a smile. "Jealously. I've always liked Devon. I fought for his attention for months, but he never did look my way. He's too in love with someone else to notice me."

"Did you tell him? How you felt?"

She scoffs, "I made an attempt, but he made it clear that his feelings wouldn't change. Last night was the first time he's acknowledged me since."

"So… you took your chance," I add, understanding her side of things.

"I should have known better, but a part of me hoped a night together would change his mind," she takes a deep breath and shrugs. "Somethings aren't worth it. Regret is shared in this instance."

"Amanda! Help us," Meredith yells from her car, parked on the street.

"I'm gonna go," Amanda gestures towards them before awkwardly rushing off.

I turn and walk back into the house, curious to where all the guys disappeared to. A few steps from the door, Devon steps around the corner from the hallway, leaning against the wall, arms crossed. "You heard?"

He nods, "Yeah, every word."

"How does that make you feel?"

"It reminds me of all the baggage I carry."

"Is that all?" I gently push.

"She's right, you know," he nods, looking down at his shoes as he stands straight, pulling his weight from the wall. "I am in love with someone else. So, although what I did was wrong, I see her side of things too. I'd have done anything to get the attention of the one *I* want attention from."

"Why don't you?"

He takes in a long, exaggerated breath, blowing it out and shrugging before verbally answering. "Love isn't easy."

Before I can push the conversation further, there is a commotion behind me as Amanda returns with Alice, Taylor, and

Meredith in tow, all carrying a huge crepe myrtle tree. They stand it up on the front porch, all stepping back to gesture with jazz hands as they all yell, "Tada!"

"And what exactly is that?" I ask, walking over to check out the six-foot tall tree with beautiful deep red flowers popping off at the end of the new growth branches.

"Your first tree for your new house!" Meredith explains in an overly excited voice.

"We told you this was an odd idea," Alice whispers from the side of her mouth while trying to disguise her feelings with a fake smile.

"It's cool, but not a normal housewarming gift," Taylor adds, placing her hands on her hips in a stance that looks more like a model pose than anything else.

"Okay, listen," Meredith steps forward as if this is her one line in the show. "It was an odd family tradition for my family. We moved around a lot. Everywhere we went, we planted a new crepe myrtle to mark it as ours," she shrugs. So, to me it feels normal. To me, it feels like home," she smiles genuinely at me.

I step forward and smile, reaching my arms out to invite her into a huge. She takes a moment to smile back and step into my arms. "It's perfect. I love the idea that it makes it feel like my home. Thank you. This is really sweet."

"Really?" Amanda asks, hands on her hips as she looks between Meredith and I as if we've each grown an extra appendage or something.

"What?" Alice asks, looking at Amanda as if she's the one who grew a second head or something.

"I just..." Amanda looks around at everyone. Before she can continue Thomas and Johnny step out onto the porch.

"What's going on out here?" Thomas asks.

"Meredith bought Gina a tree," Taylor announces, looking amused as she explains the situation.

"Now she has to find time to dig a hole, and plant it, and water it, and nurture it," Amanda begins to ramble.

"Let's show you the house and get you away from the tree," Alice suggests, putting her arm around Amanda's shoulders and ushering her inside the house.

Moments later Devon walks out. He points back inside, "What's that about?"

"Tree drama," Taylor explains vaguely.

"Alright..." Devon trails off.

"I'll help you plant the tree," Thomas randomly adds in.

"Me too," Devon agrees as he looks around for a good place. "Do you know where, or... you know what," he picks up the tree pot and carries it away from the door. "How about we just let it hangout in the shade until we unpack this trailer box thing."

"Great idea, Devon. I didn't know you could have those," Meredith says in a sassy voice.

"Wow," Jimmy says as he walks out the front door mid arm stretch. "I think I felt safer inside."

"Just the normal family drama," Taylor admits with a shrug before starting her our stretching routine.

"Where do we start?" Thomas asks with a huge smile on his face, like he's about to win a prize.

"Every box is labeled with which room it belongs to. I labeled the walls where I want the boxes. Furniture will have to be piece of piece because I didn't mark any of that.

"Alright," Robert says as he walks up toward the front porch. "You heard the women. Grab a box and get moving. Let's clear this moving trailer in record time!"

Everyone moves down the steps to the moving box trailer and begins to grab an item here and there. Once everyone got a system and a flow, the trailer began to clear out at record speed. I had to stop for a bit to get furniture situated in the right rooms, but not only did my new friends unload the trailer with me, they built my furniture and helped set up everything they could.

Once the trailer was empty, the dancers even helped me unpack the kitchen. Meredith came over to ask where I wanted certain items so that they could put a few glass items away. Alice and Taylor climbed up on the counters to wipe down every shelf and surface with cleaner before Meredith and Amanda placed anything onto shelves or inside of cabinets. Before I knew it, I had a kitchen fit to serve dinner.

∞

Pizza & Beer

The front door opening caught everyone's attention as the sun began to set outside. "Hello?" a male voice said awkwardly from the front door.

"Hey!" Thomas ran toward the door with a smile.

"I thought everyone was already here," I look at Devon in confusion as we both sit and listen for a clue.

"I heard that pizza and beer was in order," the male says.

Devon smiles as he puts the final felt pad on the bottom of my new desk. "That's just Kyle."

"Stage manager, Kyle?" I ask, surprised that he'd come to help, seeing as I'm not sure that boy ever sleeps as it is.

"The one and only," Devon nods as he stands. "Here, flip that side," he gestures to my end of the desk as we flip it and move it into place. "Done. Perfect timing."

"Thanks again," I offer before we head toward the kitchen where everyone else is gathering.

He smiles. "What are friends for?"

"You are a complicated person. You know that right?"

"So I've been told," he laughs as he steps into the kitchen. "We better go before those dancers eat all the pizza."

"There she is!" Thomas smiles and cheers as I enter the kitchen.

"Hey, Gina," Kyle says as he walks around the crowd toward me. "Welcome to your new home," he says, handing me a green house plant with long skinny leaves.

"Thanks," I smile, investigating what it might be.

"It's a spider plant," he begins. "Not like the bug. It doesn't attract them either or anything. It's just a nice simple house plant that anyone can keep alive. I figured that if you weren't a plant person, at least you'd have a chance at keeping it alive. I really didn't know what to get you," he shrugs.

"Delivering pizza and beer was enough," I laugh.

He shrugs again, "I'm used to running things and being in charge. The unknowns are what scare me and give me anxiety. What can I say? That's why I became a stage manager. Being in charge can really help sometimes."

"Well, in that case," I say, handing him one of the beers he brought, "You're in charge of the fun tonight."

"Oh snap," Devon says from next to me, covering his face like I said something wrong.

"What? What did I say?" I look around and notice everyone is avoiding eye contact.

"You thought Devon's party was wild?" Thomas asks.

"I'm tame, compared to Kyle," Devon admits.

"Okay, listen," Kyle begins. "This isn't my house. And this is a family party. I will not introduce any new friends or liquor to the house."

"Yeah, some of us are still hung over from last night," Amanda admits, glancing briefly at Devon before grabbing a beer and throwing it back as if her hangover comment doesn't apply.

"Note to self, Kyle's parties are apparently the most fun," I joke, grabbing my own beer and raising it in the air. "A toast. To all of us. To friendships new and old," I look around at everyone as I continue. "Thank you for welcoming me with open arms. Thank you for letting me in and trusting me," I glance to Amanda and Devon. "And most importantly of all, thank you for helping me unpack and make today possible. I'm not sure how I would have done that alone."

"Hear, hear," Robert yells, raising his glass.

"Cheers!" Thomas yells.

Everyone raises their glass, clinking them together before digging in to pizza and beer. We all lounge around wherever we can find a seat. The couch and love seat are placed haphazardly in the middle of the room but are just as comfortable as if they were in a permanent place.

Once everyone finishes eating, Thomas and Devon clean up as much trash as possible between the pizza boxes, wrapping materials, and cardboard throughout the house. Everyone else slowly heads home for the night, leaving the three of us alone. Devon and Thomas take the last load of trash out to Thomas's truck before returning inside.

"Are you sure you can take all that?" I ask Thomas, making sure he can really dispose of all that trash himself.

"Positive," he smiles.

"Imma head out," Devon steps forward, reaching towards me to hug me goodbye. "Welcome to the fam," he says before fist bumping Thomas and waving as he jogs out to his car. "See you two."

"He is one complicated character," I whisper without realizing I said it out loud.

"He's a good kid. He just goes about showing it in the worst ways," Thomas agrees as we watch Devon climb into his car. "I'm going to head home too. It's been a long day."

"Yeah. Last night really took a lot more out of me than I thought it would," I admit.

Thomas sighs, "I haven't spent the night at one of Devon's parties in a very long time."

"Really?"

"Yeah," he looks down. "Honestly, it hasn't felt like a family for a while. You coming here... it has brought us back together in a strange yet organic way. We're all really glad that you're here."

I smile, "Thanks Thomas. That really means a lot."

He backs up and points toward his truck. "I better head home and get some rest." He takes another step away and bites his bottom lip like he has more to say. After several more awkward moments of silence he spits out, "Goodnight!" before disappearing down the sidewalk in record time.

"Goodnight!" I yell back, surprised and confused by his sudden exit. "Drive safe! Thanks again!"

"Anytime!" he yells back before climbing into his truck and quickly driving away.

I shrug as I watch him drive away. Figuring that moment out needs to wait until tomorrow. For now, I'm exhausted, and so thrilled that Thomas and Devon assembled my bedroom before dinner. If that wasn't built, I'd probably just pass out on the floor in a pile of sheets. I'm so tired.

I lock all the doors, shut off the lights, turn off morning alarms, and pass out before I even remember pulling the covers over my face.

CHAPTER 7
RETURN TO WORK

What happens over the weekend is meant to be private recovery time. Sometimes that happens, but other times, you spend every moment with the same people you see all week. It happens with people from your hometown, people from your college dorms or course work, and of course, your co-workers. When do you take a step away from the people you see all week to just have time for yourself?

Drama can grow between friend groups and co-workers if you spend too much time together. Imagine not spending time with anyone other than the people you see on the daily? Yeah, it can lead to long lasting, strong bonds, but it can also lead to frustration and misplaced anger. It can also divide groups when love interests grow and change, often harming the group dynamic.

Back Lash

Going back to work is almost strange. Spending most of the weekend with co-workers was not something I did at my last job! It is already beginning to feel like more of a family than a job, which is nice. It also brings its share of drama, or well, it could.

"Morning," Johnny said, walking up next to me in the parking lot.

"Hey! Good morning," I reply with a smile, thankful to not have to walk in alone. The security staff still isn't used to me, so it's nice to have someone to talk to as we enter the employee entrance of the park.

"Get everything unpacked?" he asks as we step into the employee building, holding the door open for me to step inside first.

"Not everything," I admit, walking in. "Thanks, but umm the necessities are unpacked. I wouldn't have been able to do it without everyone's help!"

"Well, we are an odd group, but we're family."

"And those pastries from your wife, were amazing," I admit. "I don't think I ever liked breakfast pastries before now."

Johnny laughs, "Yeah, she sure does have a way of making a breakfast pastry special."

"Is she going to open her own shop or bakery ever?" I ask as I place my backpack onto the belt to go through the x-ray machine.

"She has considered it a few times, but she also loves being home with the kids," he shrugs. "Maybe when they're a little older and all in school, she will."

"At least she has a passion that she loves," I smile before stepping thew the metal detector and waiting for my bag at the other end.

"What about you?" he asks. "Any long-term plans to perform?"

I shrug as I reach for my backpack, now coming out of the machine. "I'm just going with the flow for now. In high school, everyone told me that I was perfect for cruise lines, you know because they do such a variety, but that just wasn't in the cards for me at the time."

"Do you regret it?" he asks as he steps through the metal detector.

"No, actually, I'm glad I didn't do it! Could you imagine if I had worked on a cruise line during Covid? I would have been stuck quarantining with all those sick people in the middle of the ocean or on the docks for weeks!"

"Yeah," he agrees, "That would have been a rough experience to endure."

"So, yeah looking back, I'm glad I didn't do it. Once we did get off the boat, we'd have been jobless for who knows how long. Everything truly happens for a reason," I shrug as I toss my backpack onto my shoulder and head towards the park.

"Regardless, we're all glad you're here," Johnny says as we step through the doors and out into the park.

"Morning," Robert says walking up to us with Jimmy not far behind.

"Morning, where have you two been?" Johnny asks them.

"Coffee," Jimmy answers, "Not like Robert needs anymore."

"What? Come on, I'm fine!" Robert tries and fails to convince any of us that he's fine.

"What's got you all worked up this morning?" Johnny asks in his normal calm demeanor, even though it would be easy to match Robert's energy.

"The tempo of that piece Jimmy's been mixing for us," Robert admits, looking even more anxious, if that's even possible.

"How long have y'all been here?" Johnny asks, looking at Jimmy with concern in his eyes.

"Would you believe me if I said five o'clock this morning," Jimmy shrugs.

"Who let you in?" Johnny asks.

"Night shift Bob," Robert shrugs three times, clearly needing to lay off the caffeine.

"Okay, why don't I carry this," Johnny says, gently taking the coffee from Robert. "And you tell me what the issue we need to fix is."

Robert starts to ramble as Johnny looks over his shoulder to smile at me before following Robert at a rushed pace.

"Sorry," Jimmy says with a shrug.

I wave him off, "No biggie."

"I'm gonna go," he gestures towards them, "and try to save Johnny."

I laugh, "I hope you succeed."

He waves as he runs off.

I look down, shaking my head. I begin walking slowly towards the theater when I hear the door close behind me. I glance back and see Devon, shades covering his eyes as he walks towards me.

"Hey Gina," he says with a cocky smile.

"Morning," I stop, waiting for him to catch up before beginning to walk again. "Late night?" I gesture to the sunglasses.

He smiles again, looking happier than I've seen him. "Nah, just a regular ol' headache."

"No shenanigans last night?" I push.

"No mother," he shakes his head. "I actually spent some time to myself and did some reflecting and thinking," he shrugs.

"Well reflection looks good on you," I joke as we round the corner to the back door, spotting Amanda and Meredith chatting in the corner.

"I am mighty good looking, aren't I?" he jokes back before he notices Amanda and Meredith are within earshot.

Amanda rolls her eyes dramatically. "It doesn't matter, just drop it," she practically growls out to Meredith before storming off into the building.

Meredith shrugs and smiles at us awkwardly before running inside after her.

"Shit," Devon whispers out.

"You think that has something to do with you?" I ask.

He takes in a deep breath and lets it out slowly before taking off his sunglasses and looking over at me. "I'm afraid they got the wrong idea." He looks at me with a serious look in his eyes, and I can't figure out why.

"Wait," I consider the jokes we were making when we came around the corner. "You don't think... you don't think they think that..." I gesture around looking for the right words.

He looks down and sighs, "I hope not, but I also know what they're like."

"Because of the last girl?" I ask about the girl I replaced.

He shrugs, "She really wasn't a problem. Nothing ever happened with us. That didn't stop them from thinking something did."

"Hey," I reach over and place my hand on his arm. "Try not to let this get to you. Talkers gonna talk crap. Drama is gonna spread, no matter what you do to stop it. We didn't do anything wrong, and that's what matters."

Just before I finish, I notice Devon's eyes go past me. I glance over and see Thomas sneaking into the back door quickly, trying to go unnoticed. "You don't think he..." I start before looking back at Devon and dropping my hand from his arm.

"I'll set it straight with him, don't worry," Devon reassures me. "He knows all my dirty secrets. He'll know I'm telling the truth when I explain everything. You have no need to worry," he smiles.

I blow out a breath. "We don't need that awkward tension to follow us on stage."

"I have a feeling a lot of that will be going around today." He steps towards the door, "Come on. We better get in there and go our separate ways before whatever they're saying in there gets worse."

"Right."

He grabs the door, holding it open for me, making me feel even more embarrassed, knowing the rumors will only get worse if someone notices the kind gesture from Mr. Grumpy.

"Thanks," I whisper as I walk inside and quickly turn down the hallway towards the coffee shop, separating myself from Devon.

"See ya later," he whispers with an eye roll.

∞

Costume Changes

Everything for the first show is pure chaos. I don't think my first day winging it even felt this bad.

"Move it," Amanda grumbled as she pushed past me while trying to pull her red costume off from over her white costume.

"Sorry," I whispered, even though I was not even close to in her way.

"Ready?" Devon asks as he lifts the curtain for my entrance from backstage center.

"Thanks," I nod as I take a breath just as the lights come on and the music starts.

When my part begins, I step out and move toward downstage center as Thomas runs up the stairs in front of the stage to meet me. Our song is about us falling in love, but I'm not feeling our connection today. It seems so forced, and Thomas isn't looking at me the way he usually does. Shit, Devon and I really fucked up. Wait, we didn't even do anything. How is this even happening?

∞

Devon is on stage playing his beautiful piano solo while the dancers are all rushing to change backstage. For the longest costume change Devon, Johnny, and Jimmy all have short solos on stage. Meanwhile, the girls are tearing their velcro costumes off and velcroing the next two layers over the final costume.

During Devon's solo, I quickly change into my next costume while swaying to his comfortable rhythm, just like I do at every show to try to ease away any lingering nerves or tension. This time, I feel four sets of eyes analyzing my every movement as if it means something more.

"Shit," I whisper under my breath as Thomas walks up beside me.

"You okay?"

"Umm, yeah. Why?" I ask, straightening my costume one last

time as we prepare to enter for the next song.

"Just heard you cussing and was worried," he shrugs.

"Just having a day," I say, glancing over at the four dancers still watching my every move while they help each other velcro on their costumes over one another.

"Ignore them. They can be really sweet, but they can also be a bunch of bitches," he jokes with a smile.

"What about you?" I dare ask.

"What do you mean?" he asks.

Before I can repeat myself, we hear his cue. He shrugs and whispers, "Later," before rushing in for his entrance.

I nod to reassure him before moving to my own entrance at the side of the stage next to Devon. Realizing the proximity, I roll my eyes and shake the stress out of my shoulders, though I feel I only make it worse.

Once I hear my cue, I step around the wall, singing as I move in behind Devon. He smiles at me as he plays through the song with ease. To the crowd he is helping build the atmosphere. To Thomas and the dancers, he is flirting. Sure, this song requires a little bit of flirting and playing a character, but it's always been an act for us. It's no different now as we flirt through the song with ease.

Partway through, Thomas enters from the other side of the stage and demands our attention. His part of the jealous boyfriend looks all too real as Devon and I feel his anger to the core of the words in the song. I quickly follow my blocking to rush over to him, but his improv proves fierce as he storms past me, careful not to make physical contact as he lives his part rather than playing the character.

As the song ends and the crowd cheers, Devon and I make eye contact. He clearly feels the same shift in our family as I do. Thomas is pissed, though I can't for the life of me figure out why.

The next song is Thomas singing while the dancers perform with him. The dancers are extra flirty and touchy feely today. I can't tell if they are playing off of his energy or their own.

"The energy around here today is odd," Johnny whispers from the stage as I look out from behind the curtain nearest to him.

"You're telling me," I whisper back.

"You okay?" he asks.

"Yeah. Fine and dandy," I shrug. Clearly, he's heard something, or he wouldn't be asking.

"If you need to talk, or help clearing the air..." he whispers.

"I'm good, really. It'll blow over," I whisper just before having to move towards my cue for the final number.

The girls all rush off stage, tearing off the overalls and checking their final costumes for the finale. I can't wait for this show to be over. As they exit, Meredith and Amanda both intentionally bump me from each side as they go by. I'm not sure why Meredith of all people is mad at me, but I've got to just ignore it for now.

Thankfully, everyone in the cast wants this performance over with. I'm not sure if the crowd feels it, but the finale was as amazing as always. It was like we were performing as if it was the real end of our group. Everyone was on their marks. Every note came out perfectly. And everyone cheered with the crowd once the final light cue drops the bow lights to zero. We all run off stage to the wings before the house lights come on for the audience to leave.

"I need a drink," I hear Amanda groan to Alice as they throw hoodies on over their costumes as they preset all of their costumes for the next show.

"Maybe we can wait for tonight?" Taylor shrugs, clearly the only sensible one in the group.

I exit the stage, glancing back to find Devon and Thomas walking out behind me. Everyone is silent for the first few steps. Once we make it down to the first set of doors, I glance back and give Devon a stern stare.

Devon lifts his hands to ward me off before turning to Thomas, "Hey man. Can we go talk somewhere for a minute?"

Thomas glances between us for a moment before replying, "Yeah, sure." As he turns to follow Devon towards the exterior door, he looks back at me for answers. I shrug before disappearing down our hallway and into my own dressing room to hide.

CHAPTER 8
CLEARING THE AIR

The human race would be boring without drama, wouldn't it? I mean, think about it, most of middle and high school is fueled by drama when students aren't learning something. When you get out of high school and move into the great big world of college, the drama gets even more real. Maybe it's less often, but when it does happen, it's even more intense. Then, in the job world, man can drama and fake news ruin everything. Everyone has an opinion, but everyone also has an assumption.

A school principal once addressed his staff, reminding them that they are not so different from the students they teach. As adults, we say we don't cause drama, but the assumptions made, and the game of telephone is a dangerous game. The worst is when someone tells their personal truth, but by the time it makes it around the school, the game of telephone has changed the entire story. Live by the fact that if you did not hear it from the source, it's probably not true or simply twisted truth by the time it gets to you. If everyone lived with that basic understanding, if everyone questioned rumors unless it came from the source, then the world would be a much better place. Maybe it would be boring, but maybe boring could be fun, right?

Assumptions

I decide to eat my packed meal now and eat dinner somewhere within the park after the next show. If that show is as toxic and tense at the first was, I'm going to need to get far away from these people for a little while to handle the third show of the day. After I finish, I pull out my notebook to start writing theme ideas for song lyrics down. Wait, is this a good idea? Are people going to make assumptions about Devon and I writing a song? No. Nope. I will not ask him for help until after this all blows over. It will blow over, right?

Before I can shake the thought, I hear a knock at my door, hoping it isn't Devon. "Come in," I yell out, not bothering to turn toward it. I left it cracked open anyways, so maybe whoever it is, is already inside.

"Hey," I hear Thomas whisper from the doorway.

I spin my chair around to face him. He looks a bit sad, honestly. He's leaning up against my door frame, arms crossed over his chest. "You okay?"

"Yeah," he nods, looking down and avoiding eye contact. "I just feel like a jerk."

"Thomas," I start, waiting for him to look up. He looks up for a moment before looking away again. "What are you talking about?"

He steps into the room and throws his arms up in the air, clearly upset about something. He closes the door behind him and begins to pace the room. I can't tell what's happening, so I let him pace until he finally stops and looks at me. "I'm a terrible human being." He sits backwards down onto my couch, elbows on his knees. He puts his hands on his face, hiding from the world.

"Thomas, that could never be true," I laugh. "Tell me what's going on. Maybe I can help?" I suggest with a shrug.

He laughs and drops his hands, leaning back and looking up at me. "I made an assumption that I can't take back and I feel awful."

"What was this assumption about?" I ask, wondering if Devon talked to him.

"You," he admits immediately. "It was about you and I feel like an idiot and a jerk."

"Whoa," I start, standing and walking over to him. "First off, I'm not even mad, about... whatever you did," I shrug. "Second, you really need to start from the beginning, because I'm lost." I plop down on the couch beside him, bending one knee to face him. "Come on. Spill." I try to remain calm and indifferent so I can hear his side of things before deciding on my feelings.

"Like you don't know," he scoffs, looking away while shaking his head.

"Humor me," I smirk.

He turns and notices the smirk. He rolls his eyes, "See! You do know."

"Well, tell me what I don't know. What made you think that?"

He sighs, "I heard y'all talking outside about whatever y'all did, there was nothing wrong about it."

"And?"

"And I assumed he checked another girl off his list," he shrugs.

I laugh out loud, "You thought I slept with him! Devon!?"

"Why are you laughing?" he looks at me with pure confusion in his eyes.

"You actually believed that just from overhearing a vague statement?"

"Well, he has a history."

"Do I fit into the category of types of people to fall for his *history*?" I ask, feeling a bit insulted.

He glances up before shaking his head and looking away. "I mean his type is simple. Female."

I laugh and he chuckles from beside me, clearly still upset with himself over nothing. "You have a point," I say to try to ease his suffering.

"You're not mad at me?" he asks genuinely, looking up with a defeated look still plastered along his face.

"Thomas," I start, reaching out to touch his arm. "Why would I ever be mad at you?"

"Because I was rude this morning for no reason! I let my emotions play into our performance. I let my friend down. I did everything wrong today."

"You're here now," I shrug.

"Is that really enough?" he looks deep into my eyes like he can tell if I tell the truth with him doing so.

"Looking from someone else's eyes, I can see how that interaction between us could be... misunderstood."

"You can?"

"Johnny asked me during the show if I needed him to help set things straight. I knew then that this was more than just a few people making an assumption about us talking."

"Well, when I saw you, you had your hand on his arm," he glances down at my hand currently outstretched doing the same thing to his arm.

"Oh, right," I say, pulling my hand back and resting it on my lap.

"Hey," he says, reaching out and taking that hand into his own.

"I didn't mean for that to come off in a negative way. I'm just pointing out that before I heard you guys talking, I walked around the corner and saw that."

"Again, I can see how that might be misunderstood, especially given his history. And I know we don't know each other that well yet, but I would hope that you'd know I'm not the kind of girl to put herself into a situation like that. At least, not on a whim so quickly."

"I do know that. I just couldn't see past my... I don't want to call it anger, but I was upset and I just couldn't see past it. It surprised me, caught me off guard, and clouded my judgement. I should have come to one of you and asked. I should have gotten the facts from one of you before taking it out on you guys."

"I'm sure the dancers talking didn't help," I shrug.

He laughs, "Yeah. They're all super pissed, especially Amanda."

"Well, that's because I told her Devon must regret sleeping with her at the party over the weekend," I admit.

"No, you didn't!"

"It kind of just slipped," I shrug.

"I love you!" he laughs. "Tell those girls."

I brush off the fact that he just said he loved me. Clearly, he means in a friendship kind of a way, right? "I don't want them to hate me because they also made assumptions though," I stand up and walk towards the other side of the room.

Thomas stands behind me, reaching out to cup my shoulder, forcing me to turn back around and face him. "Listen, this won't last. Even if I don't storm in there and explain what really happened, they'll forgive you. Shit, I bet they've all slept with Devon by now, and they've forgiven each other."

"But I don't want their forgiveness for the wrong things," I shake my head and duck out from under his hand.

"Do you want me to talk to them?" he asks.

I shake my head, "I don't think so."

"But you don't know so?" he asks, trying to make a joke and ease the tension growing in the room.

I turn and smile at his attempt to ease the situation. "I don't want to go in there and explain away an assumption. I feel like they'll think I'm lying. I don't want Johnny to tell everyone that he saw me *alone* in the parking lot and walked through security and into the park with me and only me."

"Wait, you did?" he sounds surprised.

"I thought we covered this. Nothing happened between Devon and me."

"Right, sorry."

"And..." I draw that out. "I don't want you going in there and trying to explain it all away either. You may know the truth. You may have heard both of our sides of things, but that doesn't mean you have to correct their mistakes in thinking."

"So, what did happen between you two? Like, I know you didn't sleep with him or whatever, but clearly you know something I don't. Clearly you two made a connection over the weekend."

"He opened up about some things. I'm not sure why I was the person he opened up to, but maybe it's because he knows I'm far from the type that will sleep with him," I laugh. "Anyway, his secrets are not mine to tell. He let me in on some inner thoughts about himself and the people around him, especially girls. I told him he needed to make a decision about what he wants in life."

"Wow," is all Thomas can say.

"This morning, he caught up to me before we reached the theater. We rounded the corner while making a joke and saw Meredith and Amanda arguing out back about something. They saw us and Amanda stormed off. Meredith followed with a nonchalant shrug, but that is where their rumors all started."

"Because they didn't see you come into the park with Johnny," he acknowledged his own mistake.

"Assumptions are dangerous."

"Yeah. You're right."

"So, no. I don't want you telling the dancers the truth. They need to figure it out on their own."

"Okay," he nods. "But, if things get out of hand out on that stage, I can't promise not to speak my mind."

"I can appreciate that," I smile at him, glad to have my friend back. I don't think I'd survive this place without him.

"Alright, well, I'll leave you alone until the next show," he forces a shy smile before stepping towards the door, pulling it open slowly before looking back at me. "Hey, umm."

"Yeah?" I smile.

"After the show, want to go grab a bite at one of the other restaurants? We can avoid the dancers and Devon for a little while before the evening show?"

"Sounds like the perfect plan."

He smiles genuinely for the first time today. "Great," he says before disappearing down the hall.

∞

Escalation

The second show feels better with Thomas acting like his normal self, but if it's at all possible, the dancers are ten times worse than before.

"Move!" Amanda yells every time she exits the stage anywhere near me.

"You're off key," Alice says once, rolling her eyes. I'm not sure if she is rolling her eyes at me or the fact that she is being made to say it from someone else.

"Hey. What's wrong?" Devon asks during the one song he leaves the piano. The same song that he lifts the back curtain for me.

"Nothing," I shake my head, trying to ignore it.

"Something," he pushes.

"Just the same," I avoid eye contact.

He looks at me with concern on his face before glancing back at the changing dancers. Normally he'd be gawking at their every movement while changing costumes, but he's glaring instead. "Will y'all give it a rest already! Nothing happened."

"Curtain," I hear Kyle yell through the nearby tech headset hanging on the wall.

"Curtain cue," I whisper out to get his attention.

"Oh, shit," he whispers as he lifts the curtain in a rush. "Sorry Gina," he says as he lowers it behind me as the music repeats the intro for me.

"Mind your business, Devon," Amanda yells at him. I hope the audience isn't listening in, because the band and I can sure hear every word.

"I'm trying to," Devon yells back. "You four are the ones making incorrect assumptions. Now get your heads out of your asses and go dance like professionals!"

Even while singing, I can hear their exchange, and I'm actually impressed. I see Johnny give me a smiling nod as he also heard the entire exchange even over his drum set.

When the song ends and Devon is back at his piano, the lights fade on Thomas and I as they come up on Devon for his short singing solo of the next song. He doesn't miss a beat. He actually looks more relaxed than I've seen him.

"Did I hear what I think I heard?" Thomas whispers over his shoulder as we rush off stage left, opposite Devon and the piano.

"If you heard Devon telling off the dancers, then you sure did."

"Wow. I didn't think he had it in him," Thomas admits as he tosses off his leather jacket and pulls off his velcro version of a button-down shirt.

"Yeah," I whisper as I turn to watch the dancers come out for their flirting scene with him. The tension is heavy as they are all forcing their expressions as Devon looks more comfortable than ever.

I look back at Thomas and surprise myself when I look at his fit chest and abs on full display as he pulls a navy t-shirt over his head for the next song.

"What?" he asks, looking at me like I've lost my mind. "Is there something on my face? What?" he asks as he frantically looks down at himself to be sure he isn't missing something.

"Nothing," I whisper as I rush backstage to cross to the other side to prepare for my flirt scene with Devon. Damn that's gonna be awkward.

∞

The song with Devon goes off beautifully. It feels so natural to sing along with him. Maybe everyone else doesn't understand, but I understand Devon in a way no one else here does. He doesn't know how to show his love to the one person he wants to, so he acts as the player to keep himself busy. Thomas comes alive in a different way when he enters the stage to finish out our song. The three of us have come to a silent understanding, and it is apparent throughout that entire song.

We all exit with smiles plastered on our faces as if that was the best moment of our entertainment lives. Something about it felt different. I wonder why that is.

Thomas and I go our separate ways as he has a quick costume change to sing his song with the dancers while I need time to change into the finale outfit. I'm glad this show went better than the first of the day, but I'm really not looking forward to doing it another time today, especially after Devon's little outburst with the dancers.

Just before the song ends, I move back behind Robert to avoid the dancers during their exit. Robert steps forward to give me more space in the shadow of the curtain until it's time for my cue in the next song.

Once the bows are over and the lights go out, we all run backstage. Once everyone is together, Thomas comes up behind me and reminds me, "Change quickly so we can go grab dinner." He practically yells it so that everyone can hear.

Devon smiles at me and nods, knowing better than to make a comment right now. He glances around at the four dancers. They're trying to reset their costumes for the final show, but they're all currently side-eyeing him. He follows Thomas and I out into the back hallway.

Once the backstage door closes, I look back and whisper, "If looks could kill."

"You'd be dead," Thomas adds with a laugh.

"Yeah," Devon says, glancing back. "I feel a growing target on my back. If I'm not back in time for the next show, one of them got to me," he gestures over his shoulder, looking concerned.

"We'll be sure to let the detectives know, but the show must go on," I shrug, making a joke that causes both Devon and Thomas to laugh.

"What's so funny?" Johnny asks as he exits the stage into the hallway.

"Oh, nothing," Thomas begins, but starts laughing again.

"We were just saying that if Devon disappears before the next show, we can let the detectives know our theories, but the show must go on," I smile, trying to suppress my own laugh.

Johnny rolls his eyes before walking past us towards the band room.

∞

A few minutes later I'm rushing out to the hallway in shorts and a navy t-shirt to meet Thomas for dinner. When I reach the main hallway, Thomas and Devon are both leaning against the wall and talking.

Thomas stands up when he notices me coming toward them. "Ready?"

"Ready," I smile.

Before we can walk away the dancers all exit the backstage door.

"Timing," Devon whispers while rolling his eyes.

"Goodluck," I say with a sarcastic smile.

"Watch this," Thomas whispers to Devon before he throws his arm over my shoulders, pulling me close. "Ready for dinner babe?"

I swat at his chest as I laugh, knowing he's helping to put on a show.

"You two have fun," Devon smiles as he walks off towards the band room before the dancers can catch up to him.

"Did Thomas just call Gina... babe?" I hear Alice whisper to the other dancers as we walk out the back door together.

Once we're outside and the door closes, I shove Thomas away and laugh. "Great! Now they're going to be talking about me more."

"Oh, come on. It was just for show," Thomas grins, happy with himself for that performance.

"Your performance was abysmal at best" Kyle says under his breath as he walks by without taking his eyes off of his cellphone.

After a few moments of watching him walk away, Thomas and I make eye contact before dying laughing together.

CHAPTER 9
GETTING SERIOUS

What is the difference between your boyfriend/girlfriend and your best friend? Are they the same? Are they different? Where do we cross the line? When do people go from besties to more? Is there a real answer?

Why is it that so often, one person falls in love, while the other goes on living their life in total oblivion? There are those times when one person is just missing all the social queues. Other times, one person is so unsure of themselves, they don't even know what they want. Then, there are times that they're too busy pushing everyone away to notice that something great is right in front of their face!

Dinner

The Lion's Den was not some romantic sit-down restaurant. In fact, I'd hardly call it a restaurant. There were no servers to refill your drinks and take your empty plates. There was no wait staff shuffling around, waiting to address your needs. Nope. This was a get your food from the counter and fight for a seat type of joint. Thankfully, the dinner crowd is always way smaller than the lunch crowd.

"Here we are," Thomas places a tray overflowing with food on the table, sliding it completely on before sliding into the seat across from me. "Lemon-Lime soda" he says, taking a cup off the tray and sliding it over. "Chicken tenders, fries, BBQ, and buffalo dip," he says as he takes each item off the tray, placing them in front of me. "And chocolate cake," he finishes with a smile as he stabs a spoon into the cake.

"I see why you come here for dinner," I look around at all the food, knowing I won't eat it all.

"This place has the best portion sizes, especially for those of us working here who need the extra nutrition," he laughs. "Plus," he leans in to whisper, "Once you get to know the kitchen staff, they hook you up with all the fresh goodies."

"Ahh, I see what's really going on. You come here for the anti-food poisoning," I nod, looking around in understanding.

"Don't come here during lunch though," he shakes his head as he pulls his items off the tray so he can place it on the end of the table, away from us. "During lunch this place is stupid busy, kind of like how our crowds are when it's storming outside."

"This place doesn't look big enough to handle that," I look around realizing that it's slow in here, but most of the tables are still full of people eating and relaxing.

"It's not," he says between bites. "And the kitchen staff during lunch is really slow. I don't mean to sound hateful, but it's bad."

"It can't be too bad," I shrug before dipping my chicken in the buffalo sauce and taking a bite of the freshly made tenders.

"Listen," he leans forward again. "The day of my interview, they gave me a dining pass to check out the park for free for the day. A storm was getting close, so I ducked into here and got in line long before they shut down rides and everything. I waited in line for thirty minutes to get chicken tenders."

"Before the storms and crowds?"

He nods while chewing, then begins to explain. "This lady, she was super short, and she honestly looked frail. But," he shakes his head, "anyways, she was moving like the speed of molasses. When I got to the counter and it was my turn, she stopped to top off fries and tenders. I stood there watching here for, no lie, seven minutes."

"You're over exaggerating!"

"I wish I was." The serious look in his eye tells me he is in no way lying.

"Dang."

"Right!" he laughs. "So, I think the worst is over. I go to the checkout line thinking; hey I got this dining wristband. They're gonna scan it and I can go. Nope."

"No?"

"I waited another ten minutes in line. Remember those fresh tenders? Cold by the time I got out of the line."

"But how?" I shake my head, at a complete loss. I glance back at the lines and see no one waiting. How can this be so different.

"This girl did not talk. We all thought she was mute. She did finally talk to her boss saying she really needed to leave on time."

"Did they tell her to speed up?"

He laughs and shakes his head as he takes a sip of his drink. "They just said they'd deal with it," he waves his hand to change topic. "When I finally get to the register, I'm like here, scan my wrist band... but no... she had... to select... every... single... item... on my tray... one... at a time."

"Is it not like a simple, click, click?"

"Oh, no. It is. I watched her agonizingly looking to find each item. I wanted to physically jump the counter and do her job so the now hundreds of people in line could eat. Because now, of course, they were shutting down rides, and everyone was swarming indoors."

"She then tried not to give me a drink cup. Oh, and the fountain drinks were all messed up. None of them tasted right. But since you can't refill dining cups, you needed to *pay* if you wanted a new one," he rolls his eyes. "I feel the frustration now just remembering that day."

"What a first impression," I shake my head at the thought.

"I almost turned down the job when they offered it to me."

"Did you explain that to them?" I ask curiously.

He smirks, "I sure did. I told them every detail."

"How'd they react?"

"They were livid!" he laughs. "I swore, I thought they'd brush it under the rug, but when they heard it all, they were fuming. They called in so many different managers and administration staff for the park to hear my story."

"Dang. You were mighty important that day," I smirk, wondering if it all went to his head.

He scoffs, "Shesh, I wanted nothing to do with all that. It made me feel so uncomfortable and kind of used. I mean, don't get me wrong, things needed to change," he eats another fry before continuing. "Could they not just do their own jobs and see that there was a problem before I got here," he shrugs. "I don't know, but, I didn't like it."

"But you still took the job," I shrug, dipping my fry into his ketchup before popping it into my mouth, not even considering if he'd be okay with that. When he didn't acknowledge it, I worried less, hoping it was alright.

He shrugs, avoiding eye contact. "Not at first."

"Wait, really," I place both of my hands down on the table in surprise, leaning forward to hear more. "What happened?"

"I told them I needed to think more about their offer. They continued to call me daily promising me more and more, begging me to accept."

"What deal did you finally make?" I ask, needing to know what he got out of this.

He smirks, leaning back in his chair and crossing his arms, but the facial expression says he was a boss about whatever he asked for.

"Tell me already!" I practically yelled, looking around to see if I drew any attention, but no one is looking at us.

"I got us more funds and huge pay raises," his smirk grows, if that's even possible.

"Wait! You're the reason the show has such a huge budget? No way! You did all that?" I practically leap off the chair, trying to contain my surprise.

He shrugs it off, acting like it was no big thing.

"That's a huge victory for this show, this team!" I'm full of hope and I sound like an overly dramatic commercial character right now, talking about how much I love breathing air, but I don't care. This is amazing news. "Wait, does everyone know?"

He shakes his head, uncrossing his arms and goes back to eating. "Most of them weren't around back them. Johnny, Robert, and Kyle know. Everyone else, they don't have a clue it had anything to do with me."

"And you're okay with that?" I ask, looking to see his answer in his eyes before he even voices it. I'm learning so much about him at this meal. I never imagined he was the reason we had such a high budget and salary. This money was uncalled for, especially for such a small show within a theme park.

He shrugs one shoulder, "Yeah. I mean, sometimes I wish they knew that I'm the reason we have such fantastic weekends instead of splitting up two separate casts to cover every day."

"Two casts?"

He nods, trying to chew before explaining. "Yeah, we used to rotate two casts. We'd have cast A, B, C, & D. Our group would be like cast A. There would be an entire separate cast B, a different person for every character. Then C and D would be a mix. So if I was on cast C, you'd be on cast D. The dancers would split and such with the cast B crew so that we had rotating days off." He shakes his head and waves it off. "Honestly, it was a mess. Everyone was always trying to trade days. Sometimes people messed up which cast day it was, and an entire part would be missing. It was a total cluster."

"You fixed that too?" I'm lost as to if that was a part of his demands.

"They were not initially happy about my price demands. I filled them in on how to spend the same amount of money by allowing the cast to not perform two days a week."

"They fought you'd give *everyone* the same two days off?"

"Initially," he nods as he swirls a fry in some ketchup as he continues. "I finally said; listen, fire the worst person from each roll. They flipped at that. I had to interrupt their arguing with a 'Let me finish!'" he whisper yells like he had in the meeting. "I tell them that they only need one cast. You run the same three shows a day with one cast and two scheduled days off."

"And they just went for it?"

He laughs and leans back in his chair to catch his breath. "No way! They thought I was insane!"

"What changed their minds?"

"They had some college intern run a bunch of reports on overpaying two casts. He ran reports on audience numbers every day of the week against park attendance records. Long story short, the intern proved my point. Our audience numbers were low on Sundays and Mondays, and two different casts were overkill, especially with all the no shows and missed days by several."

"So... an intern proved your theory, but how did everything change?"

"Layoffs. They claimed the park committee wanted to save money and lay off half the staff from several shows. Thankfully, they had no idea what I had done. Those that did make the cut and stayed on with me, well they reaped the benefits when they learned there was a set schedule and a significant pay increase."

"Wow."

He shrugs. "All in a days work."

My phone alarm rings before I can reply. I flip over my phone to dismiss the alarm before sighing heavily.

"We have to head back?" he asks in a dreary tone.

"Yeah. So unfortunate. I was really getting to know all your deep, dark secrets," I smirk.

"When are you going to tell me yours?" he asks as he stands and begins to pile all of our trash onto the tray at the end of the table.

"Oh. I'll never tell," I smile mischievously at him as I help him clean up.

He shakes his head with a smile on his face. "The ever-mysterious Gina."

"Gotta keep you on your toes," I shrug as he carries the tray to the trash can ahead of me.

"Do we really have to go back?" he groans as he reaches the exit door.

"I doubt the evening show would be very good without their two lead singers," I shrug as he pulls open the door, holding it for me.

"True, but we have understudies for a reason."

"Wait, who is yours?" I ask, realizing I don't have a clue.

Thomas laughs, "Devon."

"Oh snap," I stop walking. "You can't miss a show or be sick or anything anytime soon. That would just lead to more... I don't know, nonsense."

He places a hand on my shoulder to get my attention. "Gina, calm down. First of all, I don't plan on missing any shows anytime soon, or ever really. Secondly, I think we put those rumors to rest when we left for dinner."

I shove at him, remembering what he called me as he threw his arm over my shoulder. "Thanks for reminding me. I'm still mad at you," I pout, crossing my arms over my chest.

"Oh, come on. You can't still be mad," he runs up beside me and tries to unwind my arms from the tight cross I have going on.

I dig in deep, making sure he can't rip my arms from their strong hold. "I hold a grudge for a very long time, Thomas. I hope you're ready to fight for my friendship back."

"I'd do anything," he says, stopping me to look down at me, capturing my eyes with his for several long moments before I shake myself back to life.

"Race you back!" I yell as I take off at full speed back towards the theater, leaving Thomas in the dust.

∞

Evening Show

We got back a little early since we chased each other. I won, of course, but he says it was a tie. Please. I went back to my dressing room to catch my breath and grab my water bottle before meeting Thomas, Kyle, and Devon on stage for music rehearsal. Thankfully, there were not many notes from the powers that be, who apparently were at the lunch show. Their notes were mainly for the dancers to get their acts together or find another job. Though, I don't think Kyle was supposed to share those with us. We all shared a laugh, even Kyle smirked, which is something I hadn't seen yet.

Before we knew it, we were changing for the evening show to start. The girls were still not talking to me, but now it was constant curious glances rather than death stares. I honestly almost miss the death stares.

The show began better than the first two of the day. The dancers were acting like their normal selves, well on stage at least. They were still rude backstage. I catch Meredith's eye at one point. She looks like she wants to say something but shakes her head and walks away instead. I roll my eyes and move to my next entrance.

"How was your date?" Devon whispers as we wait for the cue to lift the curtain for my entrance.

"What? You know that was for show right?" I laugh.

"Was it though?" Devon asks.

"You know why he did it," I glance at the dancers over his shoulder. "It was not a real date," I shake my head.

"Are you sure it wasn't for him?" Devon asks with raised brows just as we hear the cue for him to raise the curtain.

Dang it, Devon. I step onto stage and try my best to ignore what he said as Thomas and I finish off the song.

CHAPTER 10
REALIZATION

Relationships have so many different levels. There are acquaintances, classmates, co-workers, friends, family, best friends, love interests, and so on. The levels are almost endless. Sometimes even watching actors in movies can form a relationship. You feel something so real as you watch these fictional characters portray love stories, love, and heartache. When you can relate to characters on the screen, it makes those characters memorable.

What makes a person memorable? In your real life, you form and dissolve friendships and partnerships regularly. Sometimes friendships slowly drift away due to time and distance. Sometimes you have to rip the chord and break friendships for other reasons. And… sometimes relationships surprise you. Sometimes they come out of the blue. Sometimes love stories hide right in front of your face.

Falling

Even though the day was full of strange emotions, everyone decided it was best for us to all go out together. Johnny said that I had to go when he invited me. I was surprised he wasn't rushing home to put the kids to bed, but he said after a day like this, we need to blow off steam together or the tension will fester.

When I stepped out of my dressing room, Meredith was leaning against the wall just down the hall. As soon as I came out, she stood up straight to ask if I was coming. I wonder if Johnny told her to make sure I didn't sneak out on them. But we're all here now, and the awkwardness has only grown. Not only is the tension still evident, but I'm also trying not to over analyze what

Devon said about Thomas earlier.

"Hey," Meredith says as she slides into the high-top chair next to mine.

"Hey," I reply, not realizing how zoned out I was. I wonder how long I've been sitting here alone.

"Where did Devon and Thomas go?" she asks, looking around the crowded room.

"I think they walked Johnny and Robert out. Something about a bad decision to carpool," I shrug, not really sure that I remember what was said before they walked away.

"Oh," she says awkwardly before looking down at her hands as she nervously fidgets.

I watch her for several long moments, wondering if I can trust her. I can't keep over thinking forever, or I might explode. I take a deep breath and blurt out my question before I can internally talk myself out of it. "Do you think Thomas has feelings for me?"

Her head snaps up and the surprised look on her face has me second guessing my decision to ask her. Though, maybe it was the fact that I jumped right to it rather than building up to the question.

"Sorry. Never mind. Forget I said anything," I shake my head and wave her off as I down the remainder of the drink in front of me. I scrunch my face at the taste, realizing the ice melted long ago and the last sip was terrible.

"Oh no you don't," she says as she snatches the glass from my hand and slams it down onto the table. "You're not getting out of this conversation so easily."

When I glance up, her eyes are on me. Her face is stern, staring me down like she clearly has an opinion on the situation. "What? Why is this a big deal?" I glance away to avoid eye contact.

"You can't go from Devon to Thomas," she blurts out.

I laugh and shake my head. "So, we're back to Devon."

"Obviously we're back to Devon!" she shouts. "You acted like you weren't that type of girl, then you just go and..."

I quickly cut her off, "Stop. Just stop all the nonsense Meredith. I never slept with Devon. I am his friend. There has never been, nor will there ever be, anything beyond friendship there."

"Then what were you two talking about outside this morning?"

"How he took some time to reflect on his life and what he really wants," I shrug, trying not to share his business.

"And that's you?" Meredith asks in a sassy tone.

"No! God Meredith. You're being just as bad as everyone else. This has nothing to do with me. I had just told him a few days ago that he needed to stop messing around if he wanted something serious."

"And why would you say that?" she doesn't look convinced.

"Because he said that the one person, he actually wants to have a relationship with doesn't give him the time of day. That's probably why he's always messing around and not caring."

"Who is it?"

"Not my secret to share," I immediately shut that line of questioning down.

"But you two came in together," she accuses, trying to prove her own side of the story.

"Wrong again," I lean back and cross my arms. "I saw Johnny in the parking lot. We walked in through security together. Once inside, Robert and Jimmy stole him away. A few moments later, Devon walks in and runs to catch up. We were just talking when we got to the back door and saw you and Amanda."

"And Amanda was outside complaining about Devon. Which is where the assumptions all became just false rumors," she puts it together and looks away, shaking her head. "Shit. I'm sorry Gina."

I shrug, "It wasn't intentional."

"That doesn't make it right by a long shot. I should have gone to you instead of joining in on the hate train."

"You're probably right," I smile. "But you were already trying to help Amanda get over whatever is bothering her. I understand why it happened."

"It still shouldn't have," she acknowledges as she reaches out to place her hand on my arm in support.

"Well, thanks."

She takes her hand back and raises it to get the attention of a nearby server before ordering us a set of drinks. "If what you say is true, then why was Thomas in such a grumpy mood this morning?"

"After you followed Amanda inside, Devon was worried more drama would start," I pause to look at her and she immediately looks like she feels guilty. "I told him not to worry and that we did nothing wrong. Apparently, Thomas walked by and heard the 'did nothing wrong' part while I had my hand on Devon's arm." I shrug and shake my head. "I didn't even realize I did that until I realized Thomas saw."

"And that upset you?" she asks curiously.

I nod, "I was worried that he'd also be mad at us and make assumptions."

"Which, it seems like he got over it rather quickly?" she questions.

"Devon found him after the first show to explain."

"Bros before hoes, huh?" she shakes her head, realizing how easily Devon squashed the rumors with Thomas, but he didn't even make an attempt with her and the dancers. "Why didn't Devon tell everyone first thing and get it over with?" she asks as our drinks arrive.

"Because he's hung up on one special person. And I think he was finally going to make a move and work on having a real, serious relationship with her."

"Just to clarify, it isn't me. Is it?" she asks in a sad tone, knowing she'll never be the one he wants.

"It is not you, Meredith," I admit.

"Yeah. Didn't think so," she replies before taking a rather large drink from her glass. "But, back to Thomas. When you two went to dinner, he seemed all hot and heavy for you," she smirks and eyes me suspiciously.

"He did that to try to help eliminate rumors. We were good, but him and Devon knew it was bothering me that you and the other girls were ignoring me and not giving me a chance to explain."

"But then you just asked if I thought he liked you," she states in a bewildered voice.

I put my elbows on the table and bury my face into my hands and groan. "I'm so confused."

"Why did you ask if I thought Thomas liked you, Gina?" she asks, trying to pull my arm away so that I'd look at her.

I cave, dropping my hands with a dramatic sigh. "Because during the last show, Devon asked how our date went. I said that it was all for show because of the rumors. I said it was not a date. He asked me if I thought that was true in Thomas's eyes."

"Oh, shoot. So you think Thomas wanted it to be a date. You think he likes you, and Devon knows about it." She ponders the subject silently for a minute before she looks back up.

"I thought it was just friends helping each other out."

"Do you have feelings for Thomas?" she asks.

I look away, unsure of what I feel.

"Gina?"

I look up and shrug. "I don't know. Honestly, I never even considered it until Devon said something about dinner being a date."

"Well... did you have a good time?"

"Yeah. It was great."

"Do you feel like you could be attracted to him?"

I smile awkwardly, "I mean, yeah. I guess."

"Then what's the problem?" she asks with a smirk.

"Wait. You think he likes me? You agree with Devon?"

"I mean, you two went out to dinner alone. Granted it was in the park, so not entirely romantic, but that fits in with our lifestyle," he shrugs before downing the rest of her drink.

"Slow down there slugger," Devon says as he walks up to the table, quickly sliding into the seat next to Meredith and across from me, leaving the seat between us open for...

"What are we slowing down?" Thomas asks as he slides into the empty seat.

"Meredith's gonna need a ride home if she keeps downing drinks like that," Devon points to her empty glass.

"That's it. Let's go," Meredith says as she stands up.

"Go where?" Devon asks as Meredith tries to pull him from his chair.

"To dance!" she answers, still not letting go.

"I'm gonna need at least two more drinks if you expect me to go out there and dance," Devon replies, gently grabbing onto her arms. "Please let me go Mer."

She groans, "You're no fun! Plus, we need to let these two have some alone time, right?"

"Mer, how much have you had to drink?" Devon asks, looking concerned suddenly.

"Not enough," she leans forward into him to whisper.

"Listen. How about you go dance with the girls and I'll join you after I order another drink?" Devon whispers to her.

"You promise?" she pleads.

"Promise," Devon replies.

"Okay then," Meredith says before racing off to the dance floor with the other dancers. I don't miss their heads turning our way for a moment once Meredith arrives, probably from her clearing the air about the rumors.

"What in the world did you two talk about?" Devon asks suspiciously.

I shrug, "Nothing really. I called her out for making assumptions though."

"And?" Thomas pushes.

"And she agreed they all overreacted," I answer simply.

"Right." Devon eyes me suspiciously. I guess he can see right through me.

"Another round?" the waiter stops back by.

"You okay?" Thomas whispers to me while Devon orders a drink for him and Thomas.

"Yeah. Why?" I whisper back.

"Just checking," he smiles. "You and Meredith okay?"

"Yeah," I nod. "She feels bad for being a part of the problem instead of the solution today."

"Is she drunk?" Devon asks once the waiter walks away.

"Hardly," I answer.

"She was just acting weird when we sat down," Devon shrugs.

"Yeah, she was," Thomas laughs.

"She just wants the family back together again," I joke.

The waiter drops off our drinks as Thomas says, "She's part of the problem!"

"And maybe part of the solution, too," Devon says as he looks over at Meredith.

I glance over my should and see her jumping up and down trying to get Devon's attention. "You better go," I say as I kick him under the table.

"Ow... I mean, right," he says as he stands and downs his entire drink before heading towards the dancers. "Wish me luck."

"You sure you don't need more liquid courage first?" Thomas yells after him.

"I probably do," he turns and walks backwards to reply. "But I'm already halfway there now."

"He's a mess," I whisper to myself.

"He sure is," I'm surprised when Thomas replies, having not meant for that to be heard.

"You enjoying tonight?" I ask, trying to focus my energy on him.

"It could be worse," he smiles at me as if he can't control it.

"It really could be," I nod, sipping on the drink I really don't need to consume.

"How late are you staying out?" he asks as he sips from his as well.

I sigh, "Honestly, I never wanted to be out this late on a school night."

"School night?" he laughs.

I laugh, trying to suppress a smile. "Doesn't matter what the reasons is. If I have to get up early, it's a school night."

"Cheers to that," he jokes as he holds his glass up.

"Cheers to us," I raise my glass with his. "For removing ourselves from the drama, whenever possible."

"Drama free. It's the simple way to be," he rhymes, trying to hold in a laugh.

"That was terrible and oh so very cringe."

He bursts out laughing. "Yeah, that was bad."

"The worst," I joke. We both laugh for a few moments before slipping into silence. It isn't awkward though. It's almost peaceful, being silent in his presence.

"You gonna need a ride?" he asks.

I look down at my drink, avoiding it so I can safely drive home. "I've been pacing myself, but it wouldn't hurt to *not* drive."

"This is only the second drink I've held tonight. I don't think I ever finished half of the first," he shrugs.

"Playing driver tonight?" I ask.

He glances up at me and our eyes lock in an intense moment. "I could," is all he says as he holds my eye contact. It almost feels like he's looking directly at my inner monologue instead of my eyes.

"Then take me home," I smile as I tip back the drink and chug down the entire thing. "It looks like it isn't safe for me to drive." I slam the glass back down to the table and wait to see how he responds.

"It would be an honor to escort you," he stands and sticks his elbow out for me to wrap my arm around.

I stand, wrapping my arm around his elbow. "I need to make it in one piece. I have a show, or three, tomorrow."

"I assure you, I have a spotless driving record ma'am," he jokes as he leads me towards the exit.

∞

Catching

As Thomas turns onto my street, he can no longer hide the yawns that have been nonstop since we left the club.

"You have to stop that," I say through my own yawn.

"What's that?" he asks, seeming startled by my statement.

"Yawning," I explain, covering my own with my fist.

He chuckles, "Sorry. I didn't even realize I was doing that."

"It's been nonstop since we got in the truck."

"Yeah. I guess you're right."

"Need to crash on my couch?" I ask.

"Not necessary," he shrugs it off.

"Necessary and a good idea are two very different things," I side eye him as I push for a safer plan. "Come on. You're tired. There is no reason to be risky behind the wheel when I have a perfectly good couch. Plus, I'll need a ride to work in the morning anyways."

"You have a solid argument," he glances over at me, but begins to yawn before he can argue with me.

"See!"

"Okay. Okay," he nods in agreement while yawning again. "But I'll have to run home in the morning to change before we go to work. We don't need everyone getting the wrong idea... again."

"True," I reply as he pulls into my driveway. We sit in the truck for a minute in silence.

"Ready?" he breaks the silence to ask as his hand stops on the door handle.

"I have to ask you something before we exit this vehicle."

He drops his hand as his eyebrows scrunch in together. "This sounds serious."

"Not... serious, but... important, I guess."

"Okay. Hit me," he pivots in his seat to face me better.

I pivot towards him but avoid eye contact as I try to come up with the best words.

"Gina? Whatever it is, we can figure it out. Are you okay?" he asks when I still haven't spoken several moments later.

I let out a huge breath before glancing up at him. "I'm fine. I'm just afraid that I had the wrong impression earlier, at dinner."

"What do you mean?" he asks with both confusion and concern written all over his face. It's his eyes boring into my soul that hits me in the heart though.

"Devon asked how our date went."

"He did? When?"

"During the evening show... but why didn't you acknowledge the fact that I called it a date?"

"It's just a word," he shrugs.

"Was it really just a *word* for you?" I ask in a serious, yet light tone.

"I don't know what you mean Gina," he shakes his head. I can't tell if he's genuinely confused or holding himself back.

"Did you want it to be a date?" I ask outright.

"I was just helping out a friend," he looks away and shakes his head.

"Thomas... I'm asking here. I'm *really* asking."

I give him several beats of silence before I begin to get worried. Then he breaks the silence, without looking at me. "I don't want to jeopardize our friendship."

"You won't."

He glances up and quickly looks away, biting his bottom lip in thought. "I may have enjoyed it more if it had been a real date," he says it as almost a question. As if he's unsure of his own answer.

"Why wasn't it real?"

"That's not what you needed it to be."

I take a breath and blurt it out before I allow myself time to think. "What if it's what *I* wanted it to be, but I just didn't know it yet?"

He finally looks up at me. "Really?"

I shrug, "Maybe."

"I don't want to push the subject," he looks away again.

"Thomas," I reach out and grab his hand. "It isn't a feeling that I was expecting to have. I never saw it coming. Honestly, until Devon pointed it out, I never let myself consider the possibility."

He looks at my hand holding his before he looks up and into my eyes. "What are you saying?"

"I'm saying that I'm not trying to jump into anything, but I may return your feelings," I shrug.

"And what feelings do I have?"

I roll my eyes, "Are you unaware?"

He smirks, "I'm perfectly aware of how I feel about you."

"Good."

"Good?" he seems confused at my response.

"Yeah, good. Because I can't deal with someone not fully invested in me," I try to hide the smiling working its way out.

"Are you saying..." he begins but just shakes his head like he doesn't believe this is happening.

"Maybe it isn't just stage chemistry that we have."

"Wow. I don't know what to say."

"How about you go inside and crash on my couch and we can talk more about this over breakfast in the morning?" I ask, knowing we both need some rest before we do something we'll regret.

"Deal."

∞

We barely make it inside before we're both ready to pass out. I give Thomas a blanket and two pillows before passing out on top of my bed, fully clothed.

CHAPTER 11
TWO WEEKS LATER

It's funny how everything can change so quickly. Life is created in mere moments, and it can also be taken away in the blink of an eye. Relationships can form or break in a single heartbeat. Early love is some of the most powerful medicine the doctor can order, but heartbreak is the misery most people don't deserve.

Sometimes our perfect match gets away. Sometimes we long for a relationship with someone who will forever be out of our reach. And sometimes, the right person is right in front of us and we didn't even realize it was an option. Someone has to break through those barriers to find common ground. Once everyone is on the same page, love can bloom and grow in a single heartbeat until it has a thriving rhythm.

Thomas

Two weeks ago, I never would have imagined that a routine was beginning to form. The night that Thomas slept on my couch was the beginning of a new chapter in my life. With all of the Devon drama behind all of us, we were all able to move forward, but I never anticipated the relationship that would form with Thomas.

I sit at my kitchen table as Thomas serves another homemade breakfast. He's been doing this at least twice a week since we started dating a few days after he slept on my couch.

"Eat up. We're behind schedule," he says as he holds a piece of toast between his teeth as he slides his jacket on.

"Don't rush the most important meal of the day," I joke as I finish off the last of it. I stand and bring the plate towards the sink.

"Just drop it in there. I'll wash your dishes tonight," he suggests as his anxiety about being late wins this morning.

"Who said you'll be here tonight?" I turn and put my hands on my hips.

"Well, if not, then you'll just have a sink full of dirty dishes," he shrugs as he tosses his backpack over his shoulder and begins searching for his keys.

"And you'll still be looking for your keys," I sass back as I pick them up and dangle them by the lanyard.

"How do you always find them first?" he asks as he reaches for them and I quickly snatch them out of his reach.

"Because I move them to the key tray every time you're here since that first time you lost them."

"It was one time!" he sighs as he tries to snatch the keys from me.

"And for some reason I let you back here after you tore up my living room trying to find them," I smirk.

"What can I say, we were both exhausted that night. Plus, I would have just gone home, but you insisted that I stay here on your couch," he puts his hands on his hips when I hide the keys behind my back.

"Are you complaining about the outcome?" I tease, unable to hide the smirk on my face.

Thomas leaps forward, throwing both arms around my waist to reach behind my back and grab a hold of his keys.

"Dang," I grunt as he wins this battle. Before he can pull away, I wrap my arms up and around his neck, holding him close so he can't escape.

"What an unfortunate position to find ourselves in," he smiles down at me as he tightens his arms around me, pulling me closer.

"I thought we were running late?" I look into his eyes with as much innocence as I can muster.

"Why must you ruin a perfectly good moment," he shakes his head.

"Sorry," I whisper.

"I know how you can make it up to me," he smiles as he leans down and gently presses his lips to mine.

Once he releases me, I sigh. "Too bad that's all the time we have," I whisper before pulling myself from his arms. I toss my backpack over my shoulder before glancing back at him. "Ready?"

He sighs heavily, "If I have no other choice."

"What's the matter? Apparently, you're coming back tonight to clean my dishes anyways, remember?"

"Touche mi amor," he replies as he opens the door for me.

∞

Devon

Once we've entered the park through security, Thomas and I decide to grab a coffee before rehearsal. We head over to the coffee shop, knowing someone will be in there prepping for the day ahead. It's a Saturday morning, so it should be a busy one. It being Saturday also means we're all going to Devon's tonight.

"What has Devon been up to lately?" I ask Thomas as the barista prepares our coffees.

"What do you mean?"

"Just that I haven't seen him outside of performances or rehearsals for at least a week."

"I know he was recording something with Johnny, Robert, and Jimmy last week."

"Yeah, I do remember that. I just feel like he's had himself locked away whenever we aren't all working in some way though. Do you think we should worry?"

Thomas sighs and looks to be contemplating where he stands on the subject. "I'll try to talk to him later and see if I can trick anything out of him."

"Yeah. Let me know?"

"Of course," he smiles and leans over to kiss my cheek.

The bell over the door rings, causing us both to turn. "Speak of the devil."

"The devil? Where?" Devon jokes as he looks around for the figurative devil.

"Morning," Alice says from under his arm with a shy smile.

"Oh, hey Alice," I say, trying to hide my surprise.

"I'll go order our coffees," she smiles up at Devon before ducking out from under his arm.

He reluctantly takes the arm that was draped over her shoulders away to let it rest at his side. "Don't usually see you two getting coffee this early."

"We're a bit off our game this morning," I reply.

"And you know I hate the thought of being late," Thomas

shrugs.

"To a job that we'd never get in trouble for being late unless we missed a show?" Devon asks sarcastically.

"Hey, I take my responsibilities seriously," Thomas crosses his arms.

"Yes, yes you do," Devon smirks, glancing at me.

"It appears you're finally taking some responsibilities seriously too, huh?" I ask, gesturing towards Alice behind us.

He can't hide the early love grin on his face, but he bites his bottom lip to try. "I don't know what you mean," he shrugs it off.

"But is it? Serious? No more messing around?" I whisper, needing to know if he finally told her how he feels.

He looks over my shoulder at Alice and grins even more. He looks back at me before answering. "Yeah. I finally took your advice. I told her the truth, all of it. I told her how I really feel. It took her a few days to warm up to the idea, but she's coming around."

"Coming around to what?" she asks as she walks up, handing Devon his coffee.

"Me," he winks at her.

Her face instantly turns red. "Oh," she whispers shyly.

"If he ever hurts you, we'll kill him and hide the body for you," Thomas jokes to try to lighten the mood.

"Or with you... if you prefer to have a hand in it," I shrug.

She laughs, looking a little more at ease. "Thanks."

"We're serious," Thomas says, giving her a stern look before turning it on Devon. "Don't you dare ruin this."

Devon puts his arm back over Alice's shoulders and smiles. "I'm going to do my best to hold onto this one as long as she'll have me. I'm not planning on letting go of her or doing anything to give her a reason to leave."

"But if he does," I whisper to Alice, "we've got your back."

Alice winks at me, "I'll be sure to let you know."

"Come on, we better not be late," Thomas says as he opens the door for everyone.

"We're already clocked in," Devon replies. "Therefore, we were all early."

"I like your logic," I smile as I grab Thomas's free hand as we walk towards the theater.

Two weeks ago, I never saw these two couples forming. Two

months ago, I never saw myself being happy here. But sometimes moving on a whim creates the possibility for some amazing outcomes. I wouldn't change a thing.

ABOUT THE AUTHOR

When not writing, Stefanie can be found reading, camping, hiking, traveling, stargazing, lesson planning, and teaching. She is the author of Cleanup Crew, a clean mafia romance suspense novel filled with blood, bodies, and more. She is also the author of a YA series entitled Zero Enchantment, which is filled with magical thriller storylines as the drifters fight to eliminate a corrupt organization. She lives in Tennessee with her fiancé and their three dogs.

Don't forget to tag the book in your social media review!
#ShowtimeNovella
#StefanieDiDominzioAuthor